"Do you like m...
or breaking th...

The sexual undertone of Constantine's question became quite clear. Nicole eased back enough to look into his eyes, her body heavy with desire, her nipples tightened with arousal. "I most definitely make the rules," she whispered.

His expression held a challenge, a look that said she was wrong. A look that said *he* made the rules.

"Breaking the rules," he said, his voice stroking her nerve endings, "can be quite...enjoyable."

As if to prove his point, Constantine's hand inched up her thigh beneath the red tablecloth. He caressed and teased her sensitive flesh. Nicole sucked in her breath.

"I don't break the rules," she managed, her hand sliding beneath the table to still his. "But I make the people who do, pay for their bad behavior."

"Really?" Constantine asked, interest lacing his tone. "A real good girl, are you?" He nudged her legs a bit farther apart and settled his forehead against hers. When he spoke, his voice was soft.

"You aren't such a good girl right now, Nicole...."

Blaze

Dear Reader,

Recently I loaded everything I owned into a U-Haul truck and moved from Texas to New York. Leaving Texas had me replaying in my head all the things I was going to miss about my home state. After a few months of living in New York, I have found new things to love here, but I miss much about Texas.

I especially miss those red-hot cowboys. Love them cowboys. Everything about them—snug jeans that hug their muscular thighs, hats that tilt back just the right way to complement cocky attitudes that say they know all the right moves at all the right times. Oh yeah. Love those cowboys.

And you know, one thing about a cowboy—a *real* rough-and-tough cowboy—is that he is always guaranteed to be a wild ride. And if there is any cowboy who truly fits that bill, it's Constantine Vega, my hero from *Lone Star Surrender*. He's dangerous. He's daring. He's *oh so* sexy. So buckle up and enjoy Constantine—I know I did!

Sincerely,

Lisa Renee Jones

Lone Star Surrender
LISA RENEE JONES

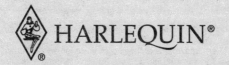

HARLEQUIN®

TORONTO • NEW YORK • LONDON
AMSTERDAM • PARIS • SYDNEY • HAMBURG
STOCKHOLM • ATHENS • TOKYO • MILAN • MADRID
PRAGUE • WARSAW • BUDAPEST • AUCKLAND

Recycling programs
for this product may
not exist in your area.

ISBN-13: 978-0-373-79446-1
ISBN-10:   0-373-79446-0

LONE STAR SURRENDER

Copyright © 2009 by Lisa Renee Jones.

ABOUT THE AUTHOR

Lisa lives in New York, where she spends her days writing the dreams playing in her head. Before becoming a writer, Lisa lived the life of a corporate executive, often taking the red-eye flight out of town and flying home for the excitement of a Little League baseball game. Visit Lisa at Lisareneejones.com.

Books by Lisa Renee Jones

HARLEQUIN BLAZE
339—HARD AND FAST

HARLEQUIN NOCTURNE
THE BEAST WITHIN
BEAST OF DESIRE
BEAST OF DARKNESS

To Janice for the insight and support that makes me so much better. To Diego for being the light that lifts me up. To my Mom and kids for always believing in me.

And to my Red Hot Readers—
you guys are wonderful!

1

HEAT. DESIRE. ATTRACTION.

He watched her from across the ritzy Hyatt Regency Hotel bar, his attention riveted by her every move. Her every nuance. The sultry beat of a slow song filtered through the smoke-filled bar, echoing the thrum of awareness dancing through his body. She shifted in her chair, her baby-blue skirt riding high…exposing long, sexy legs.

Legs he'd love to have wrapped around his waist, her body pressed close.

His reaction to his target, the woman he'd been following for two days now, came as a surprise. He didn't normally find his work distracting. But a woman like this one could make a man forget that business and pleasure didn't mix. She could make a man debate the merits of crossing the line to do things he might later regret. A line he had no intention of crossing.

Nicole Ward sat among a group of people, all there to congratulate her sister, Brenda, for passing the bar exam. His target's sleek blond hair still in the prim-and-proper knot she wore at work. He wondered what it took to get her to set it free, to let the *woman* run wild.

The idea of finding out appealed to him far too much.

He suspected she allowed the world to see only

certain parts of her life. To see the uptight federal-prosecutor persona who lived for her job.

Even there, amongst a crowd, with a celebration underway, she remained reserved and well in check. There had to be another side to her…one she kept concealed. Perhaps too carefully. Perhaps hiding something she didn't want explored.

Which was why he was here.

He intended to find out what was beneath her exterior.

Constantine Vega knew everything that a file could tell him about Nicole Ward, down to her shoe size. Seven. Narrow. She took two creamers in her coffee and drank at least three cups each morning, in place of breakfast, but not until she completed an hour in the gym.

She'd come straight out of the University of Texas here in Austin to work for her father's law firm—a firm where decisions were made based on money, not justice. A job she'd excelled at.

Shortly after joining the law firm, she'd married her father's young protégé, Mike Parker. Divorced a year later, she took back her maiden name, and left the firm to join the U.S. Attorney's office, and now fought for people rather than power and wealth. From his observations, thus far, he thought that was true, but he had to know for sure.

After all, this blond beauty could very well hold his life in her hands. In just a few days, she'd know what few did—that he wasn't the drug lord Alvarez's right-hand man. What he was, was an undercover FBI agent who'd spent the past few years with Alvarez, preparing to take him down.

Alvarez could control people in high places; the mighty dollar, his weapon. Ironic, considering it was also the weapon of choice that Nicole's father and ex-husband had chosen. When money didn't work, Alvarez could find other ways to be persuasive. Constantine had to be sure Nicole couldn't be influenced by money, as she once had been.

Tomorrow his team would arrest another big player in the cartel, and with that takedown, Constantine's cover would be blown. Not a minute too soon, either. Just in time for him to testify against Alvarez. Although the cartel would see him dead before that happened…if given the chance.

Constantine chugged his beer with that thought, images of some of the things he'd seen, some of the things he'd done, twisting his gut. Hating himself for the blind eye he'd turned to so many wrongs.

But it was all for the greater good, he reminded himself, setting his bottle down and swallowing the bile forming in his throat. He'd made choices he wasn't proud of in order to save thousands. A few sacrificed to save many. The problem was, he wasn't so sure he believed that what he did made a difference anymore.

He'd lost too much. Gambled too much. There was just…too much.

The final cards would be played soon.

Glancing at Nicole Ward, he took in her innocent looks. Ah, but he'd seen devils who looked like angels. He had a way of getting people to share their secrets, of getting them to talk. A little sweet talk and a smile, and he'd either confirm her honesty or expose her nasty side.

He watched as she sipped from her second Tequila

Sunrise. The "ice princess"—as she'd been nicknamed by the federal investigators who couldn't score with her—had broken her own one-drink rule. Did this mean she was feeling good?

Ah…but he didn't believe she was cold, this one. Not at all. Constantine had seen her ex-husband's file. The man had a thing for kinky sex clubs and a variety of women. A habit that dated back to his married days.

Either a naughty side lurked beneath Nicole Ward's conservative exterior, or she'd been burned badly when she'd learned of her ex's habits and gone into withdrawal. Constantine's gut said she had a well-concealed kinky side. And his gut had never steered him wrong before.

If ever he'd seen a woman in need of some loving, it was this one. She was wound tight and ready for release. He could tell by the way she crossed those gorgeous legs and let her shoe dangle from her foot. He bet that her toenails were painted red, not some soft pink-and-cream color. Red for seductress. A seductress who hadn't come out to play in a very long time.

An innocent game of flirtation would get him past her defenses. Too bad he'd have to stop at a bit of wordplay. Even at that, if Nicole was, indeed, innocent of wrongdoing, she'd be mad as hell when she met him again— as her new witness. When she calmed down, she'd understand. She had to. He'd acted out of necessity, faced with what might be a decision of life or death…his.

Constantine shoved off his bar stool, and started walking toward his target. A long time ago, he'd learned to never look back.

Tonight, he would play the game, consequences be damned.

"I SHOULDN'T BE HERE," Nicole said, raising her voice to be heard over the familiar pop tune the DJ played. "I have a trial starting in less than a week."

Brenda sipped from her straw. "This night is big for me, so you will just have to deal with it. Besides," she added, "it's about time you had fun." She waved two fingers at an all-American-looking, football type across the bar. "Oooh, he's cute."

"Enjoy him, now," Nicole said, wishing Brenda would take a different path. She'd been trying to convince her to rethink her plans for months. "Going to work for Daddy means you have no life."

Brenda snorted. "Unlike you, I'm not giving up sex. I don't need a relationship, but, *honey,* I need a good man and I need one often."

"Right," Nicole said with disbelief. Brenda really didn't get how their father's world would consume her. How it could destroy her individuality and steal her life. "You'll be so buried in work, you won't remember what goes where. Sex will be a distant memory."

"You and Mike seemed to find time for sex. I seem to remember a laundry list of places you 'did it.' The storage room, the elevat—"

"Enough!" Nicole said, hating that subject. Even after three years, thinking about what she'd allowed herself to become still bothered her. "Don't remind me about Mike."

"Don't avoid the subject," Brenda retorted. "You and Mike might not have talked, but you had lots of sex, despite working at Daddy's firm. You found time and so will I. Admit it. You know it's true."

Nicole took another long sip from her straw, suddenly needing a drink. *Yes,* she'd had lots of sex with her ex. *Too* much. It had controlled her, just as money had. "Life is not about sex. That's my point." Silently she added, *Or money, as Daddy would have you believe.*

"Aha," Brenda said, crossing her arms in front of her chest and nodding as though in mock cross-examination of a witness. Her baby-blue eyes sparkled with mischief. "So you *were* having lots of sex."

"That's all I had with Mike," Nicole replied dryly.

"I see." Brenda pursed her lips as she reached for her Tequila Sunrise. "He was one of *those.* I figured as much."

Nicole's brows inched upward. "One of *those?*"

"You know," Brenda said. "The 'fuck you and roll over' types."

Running a finger over the rim of her glass, Nicole pondered her response, seeing no reason to hold back at that point. "Actually, he was the 'fuck me three times and roll over' kind of guy."

They shared a laugh and suddenly, having spoken the painfully true words out loud, Nicole felt better.

With a new, more relaxed mood, Nicole enjoyed a playful conversation with Brenda, even finding humor in her sister's ongoing flirtation with the jock guy.

Finally, when Brenda had teased the man enough, he sauntered over to the table. When the jock asked Brenda to dance, she accepted, and then cut Nicole a look. "I'll be back." She pinched the straw in Nicole's Tequila Sunrise and leaned close to her ear. "S-e-x. I need it and so do you. Find you some, honey."

Nicole cast a wry glance at the ceiling as Brenda scurried off to the dance floor, her hand in the jock's. A second later, as if he'd been beckoned by Brenda's naughty intentions on her sister's behalf, a stranger appeared.

And what a stranger he was. The man could heat an iceberg.

Shoulder-length raven hair, with a slight wave, framed a square jaw and high cheekbones. Chocolate-brown skin and a dark goatee spoke of a Hispanic heritage; the indentation in his chin and the small scar above his full top lip, of a renegade.

"Hello," he said, his voice hard to make out over the music.

But she didn't need to hear him. Her gaze locked with his, and the impact was nothing short of explosive. Awareness sent a rush of heat straight between her legs. Awareness that spoke of the kind of instant attraction rarely shared between strangers. Potent. Electric.

She swallowed hard, looking into deep, dark eyes. Dim light hid their exact color but, again, it didn't matter. They were soulful. Rich with mystery and seduction, perhaps a hint of danger.

Before she knew his intentions, he closed the distance between them, kneeling down beside her. With her legs crossed, her knee was angled toward him. His gaze dropped to the sandal dangling from her toes, and then did a slow glide up her calf, leaving goose bumps in its wake.

When his eyes lifted, his lips hinted at a smile and one right dimple. "Nice color," he said, glancing at her ruby-red toenail polish.

She uncrossed her legs, feeling amazingly aroused by something as silly as a man noticing her toenail polish. If he was this detailed in his observations out of bed, well, she couldn't help but wonder what detail he'd manage *in* bed.

Tugging on her slim blue dress, she pushed her knees together, despite an incredible yearning to simply spread them for this stranger. Compliments of the intense scrutiny she'd just endured from those seductive eyes of his, she could distinctly feel the gathering of wetness on her panties.

The man got her that ready, that fast.

It's what she called talent, because no one had done that to her in a very, very long time. So long she'd started to wonder if her sexuality switch had been flipped to a permanent off.

He inched forward, still kneeling, now so close he could lean in and be touching her. She wanted him, too. Almost as much as she wanted to reach out and feel the silky strands of his hair.

He offered her his palm, but the invitation of more sizzled in the air. "Dance?"

Her gaze dropped to his hand. A strong hand with long fingers. A hand that could be gentle and forceful. A hand that could deliver both pleasure and pain. And for the briefest of moments, she wondered what his hands would feel like on her body. Relax, she told herself. Enjoy this brief interlude. *Enjoy.*

"No name?" she asked, a playful note in her voice matching how she was feeling. "No introduction? Just straight to the dance floor?"

His hand settled on his leg and her gaze followed, a quick summation of his appearance in progress. Black boots, black slacks. Her eyes traveled, heart racing as her attention skimmed his midsection, his zipper. She swallowed hard and jerked her attention upward, away from the temptation, to his matching V-neck sweater that stretched snugly over a nice, broad chest. He was nothing like the men in her world in their conservative suits and ties, and she liked it. She liked it a lot.

Suddenly, his cheek was next to hers, the warmth of his body surrounding her. "The name is Constantine," he whispered seductively, drawing her attention back to his face. To the dimple in his chin and his dark, mesmerizing eyes. He offered his hand again. "Now we dance?"

She should say no. She didn't have time for sex games and drama. She'd seen what they did to her ex and had almost done to her. How they distorted perceptions, shifted priorities. But then, this was nothing more than a simple dance, a fun diversion that meant nothing. It was crazy to think she couldn't have a little enjoyment without losing touch with reality.

Nicole slid her palm against Constantine's, suppressing a shiver as he closed long, sensual fingers around hers. "Now we dance," she declared.

2

NICOLE WARD made him hot. Plain and simple. Far more than he'd expected at a distance.

And with her soft curves pressed against his body, swaying to the rhythmic beat of a slow song, dangerously hot possibilities played in his mind. To say he was aroused would be an understatement. He was aroused all right, cock stiff, hands burning for exploration.

She was a petite little thing, and his chin easily rested on her head; he inhaled the floral scent of her hair. Jasmine, he decided, with just a hint of vanilla. Would her skin smell like that, too?

Suddenly, the dance floor was far too crowded. Bending at the knees, he nuzzled her neck and ear, and then whispered, "Let's go to the lobby bar where we can…talk."

She flexed her fingers on his chest and then tilted her chin up to look at him, her eyes probing, intent. Finally, she eyed the table she'd been sharing with her sister. Following her lead, he eased her around for a better view, still working with the flow of the music.

Table confirmed empty, Brenda nowhere to be found, Nicole pushed to her toes, whispering in his ear, as he had hers. "Just talk, right?" she asked, easing back onto the balls of her feet to look into his face, her eyes probing his. Hesitation fanned her delicate features.

He'd asked her to the bar, not to bed, though he'd prefer the latter. A warning went off in his head—the bold attorney who charged at a drug lord was hiding from him. Why? Suspicion flared. What was she afraid of? Her own secrets? Someone else's?

Concerned he might spook her if he pushed, he winked, and held up two fingers. He needed to get past her walls, to reassure himself of her innocence. "Just talk. Scout's honor."

She let her brow inch upward as if she didn't trust his vow. He laughed. "Okay, so I was never a Scout," Constantine admitted. "I thought about it, though. Does that count?"

"Not really," she said, her expression serious. Then, she smiled, the tension from moments before fading. "But I'll accept it anyway."

She had a beautiful smile, he realized. One he'd seen rarely in the past few days of watching her. Why was that? He found himself determined to find out. Protectiveness flared in him. He told himself it was duty, honor. Nothing more. Taking her hand, he led her through the crowd. They cleared the exit and stepped into the modern-looking lobby. Abstract paintings filled the walls with splashes of red to accent the matching chairs.

Constantine turned to face Nicole, startled by what he found. Light illuminated Nicole's ivory skin and deep blue eyes. A cuty pointed chin and heartshaped face spoke more of an angel than the tough-edged prosecutor she showed the world.

His gaze dropped to her red-stained lips. Red that said, kiss me. He wanted to kiss her. No. He wanted to take her to his room and lick every inch of her body. Which wasn't an option. That would be going way over the line, and he knew it.

"You didn't tell me your name," he said, hating the charade he had to play. He lied in his world all the time, as part of his job, his cover. But Nicole wasn't like the criminals he locked away. He'd have to face that later…along with his lies. Though what options did he have? He had to evaluate her, to do his best to know she wasn't compromised by Alvarez's influence before he revealed his identity. His life depended on it.

"I guess I didn't tell you my name," she said, smiling again. "But then I don't remember you asking."

"I'm asking now," Constantine said, his brow inching upward when she didn't immediately answer. "Is it a secret?"

"Nicole! There you are!" Constantine turned to see Brenda rushing forward, an athletic-looking guy by her side. Constantine eyed Nicole. "It's not a secret anymore," he said, flashing her a grin. "Nicole."

She laughed and focused on her sister. "I was just getting some air."

Brenda detached herself from her man and went to Nicole's side, giving Constantine a blatant once-over. "I see why." Still inspecting Constantine, she said to Nicole, "I'm headed out." She dragged her gaze back to her sister's. "Looks like you don't need me."

Constantine couldn't believe his luck. With Brenda out of the picture, he would have Nicole all to himself.

Unfortunately, Nicole didn't seem to share his opinion. She snagged her sister's arm and eyed Constantine. "This is my sister, Brenda, and we need to talk." She held up a finger. "Be right back."

Constantine exchanged a quick glance with Brenda's date for the night, a guy who looked barely old enough to be inside the bar. They both shrugged and turned their attention to the ladies.

Constantine noted the stern look on Nicole's face and knew what she was saying to Brenda. She was warning her to be careful about strangers. Constantine agreed, and couldn't help but think well of Nicole for being so caring.

Nicole's expression turned softer, and Constantine saw her transform from tough older sister to a nurturing one, reaching out and brushing hair from Brenda's eyes before planting a kiss on her forehead.

His chest tightened at the display, an old emotion he'd thought buried flaring inside him—the pain of losing his younger brother a year before. He had died in the line of duty, killed by a perp who'd gotten off on a technicality. Constantine had been undercover with Alvarez then or he'd have seen justice done.

Facing his loss and the failure of the system, Constantine had wondered at his own career choices, and the price they demanded. He shoved away the thought as Nicole and Brenda approached, clearly done with their talk.

A few mumbled goodbyes later, Constantine and Nicole stood alone again, except that Nicole's mood had shifted to one of retreat, not surrender, her arms crossed protectively in front of her body.

"I, ah, better go, too," she said. "I have to work tomorrow."

Constantine narrowed his gaze on her, knowing he couldn't allow her to leave, not until he knew more about her. But there was a deeper reason, one he felt on a personal level.

He glanced at his watch. "Tomorrow's Saturday."

"I still have to work."

"Have one drink with me," he offered. "I'm only here for the night. We won't get another chance."

The words lingered between them, true in more ways than she could possibly know, heavy with the implications they held. Her lashes fluttered, shielding her eyes from his view. He could almost feel her internal struggle. Almost taste her desire.

"One drink," she finally agreed, fixing him with a smoldering hot stare. A stare that told him he could have more than a drink.

And Lord help him, he wanted more. This night could end only one of two ways. If she were on Alvarez's payroll, he'd have her naked in all of two heartbeats. But if she weren't working with Alvarez, which he strongly suspected to be the case, he'd be taking one hell of a long, cold shower.

SLIDING INTO the corner booth of the deserted lounge area, Nicole felt the flutter of anticipation in her stomach as Constantine settled in beside her.

"Tequila Sunrise?" he asked, flagging the waitress, who quickly found her way to the table.

Nicole nodded, surprised he'd noticed her drink, but pleased. Pleased to the point of feeling…aroused. Actually, everything about the man did that to her.

He ordered the drinks, and Nicole studied him. He had a strong profile, a straight nose, a solid set to his jaw that spoke of confidence, full lips meant for kissing. Her gaze slid to his hands. What was it about his hands? Strong with long fingers.

It had been forever since she'd had this kind of

reaction to a man, and she wondered, why now? Why this man? Not that he wasn't hot. He was. In fact, his body, his good looks all but screamed "sex." Still, she'd met plenty of good-looking guys. Until this man, though, she'd felt pretty darn cold. Really, truthfully, work had ruled her world, and she liked it that way. It was safe, free of emotional baggage, free of distractions.

Nicole let a slow trickle of air slide past her lips as her eyes settled on the candle flickering in the center of the table. She didn't know the answers. What she did know was that when a man could make a woman burn without even trying, she'd be in trouble when he turned up the heat. Maybe it was the setting. Or maybe her body was rebelling against the complete lack of male attention she'd imposed on it ever since her divorce.

She'd left her past behind, and sex had been a part of it. A part of the greed that had led her into a dark place she didn't want to go back to. Her stomach clenched as she thought of the case that had changed her life. Of the murderer she'd gotten off only to see him kill again. It had been a wake-up call beyond her years—a crime in and of itself.

Only recently—after putting away as many criminals as she had—had she begun to look at herself in the mirror again. To accept the past and allow herself to live again. Even so, it didn't stop her shame. Her total hatred of what she'd allowed herself to become. But it was long ago.

She was drawn to him in a way difficult to ignore. Maybe it was time to stop running and face the final part of letting go of the past. Maybe it was time to enjoy a little sexual exploration without fear.

"Finally alone," Constantine said as the waitress departed, turning a mind-melting smile on Nicole.

Dark and deserted, the lounge certainly qualified as offering privacy. Apparently, the louder bar they'd left was the popular spot for the night.

Nicole commented, quick to busy herself in conversation rather than naughty fantasies about an upstairs hotel room. "What brings you into town?"

"Business," he said. He paused, reaching for her hand and enclosing it in his.

The waitress set the drinks on the table. "What kind of business are you in?" Nicole asked, telling herself she cared about the answer, knowing she should. But she really didn't want to talk at all. She wanted to kiss him. Or just go to his room. The thought, unbidden, confirmed what her body already knew. She had to have this man.

"I'm in imports and exports." He paused, and his voice lowered, lifting her hand to his mouth, and fixing her in a sultry stare. "Unfortunately, I rarely find my way to Austin."

She swallowed, staring into those sultry eyes and feeling lost, sinking deep into the haze of attraction. In the far corners of her mind, his words still registered. Hearing that she'd probably never see this man again delivered a tiny jab of disappointment, but it also offered freedom. Freedom to explore without fear of being connected to the U.S. Attorney's office, prosecuting one of the biggest drug lords in existence. It was a rare chance to test the sexual waters again without a tomorrow to face.

"So you're staying in the hotel?" she asked, her gaze never leaving his.

His eyes darkened ever so slightly, a reaction to the implication of her question. "I am. You?"

"No. I came for a celebration," she said. He still held her hand and his thumb stroked her wrist, sending darts of heat up her arm. "My sister passed the bar exam."

His brow inched upward. "Impressive. An attorney. Does it run in the family?"

"I guess you could say that. I'm an attorney. My sister is going to work at my father's firm."

"You don't work there?"

"Ah, no." Too late—she realized how sharp the answer came out.

Judging from the look of interest on Constantine's handsome face, he hadn't missed her tone. A couple, arms around each other, walked by and Nicole was darn glad for the diversion. This was a sexy fling, not a place for dirty laundry.

Constantine let go of her hand to reach for his drink, and Nicole felt the loss of his touch instantly. She busied herself by reaching for her drink and taking a long swallow, a bit taken aback by her reaction to this man.

Constantine took a swallow from his longneck beer. "What kind of law do you practice?" he asked.

"Criminal."

"Which side?"

She tilted her head at the odd question. "What do you mean—which side?"

Just a hint of a smile played on his lips before he lifted his beer and took another drink, apparently not in a hurry to respond. When he set the bottle down, he scooted closer to her, molding their legs together, and resting his arm on the booth behind her.

He enclosed her with his body, in the intimate way

a lover encloses his woman, framed her, hiding her from the rest of the room. "Do you get the bad guys off or put them behind bars?"

"I'm a federal prosecutor," she said, certain the simple declaration would end the strange direction of the conversation.

His free hand settled beneath the hem of her skirt, resting on her knee. Tipping his head downward, Constantine's lips lingered just above her ear, his warm breath caressing her neck and sending a shiver down her spine.

"Do you like making the rules...or breaking them?" he asked.

The sexual undertone of his question became quite clear. Nicole eased back enough to look into his eyes, her body heavy with desire, her nipples tightening with arousal. "I most definitely make the rules," she whispered.

His expression held a challenge, a look that said...she was wrong. A look that said *he* made the rules. "Breaking the rules," he said, in a voice so sultry, it stroked her nerve endings and further drew her under his spell, "can be quite...enjoyable."

As if to prove his point, his hand inched up her thigh, beneath the red tablecloth, to touch her lap. He caressed and teased her sensitive flesh, *so* close to her core. So close... She sucked in a breath as his fingers brushed the damp silk between her thighs.

"I don't break the rules," Nicole managed to respond, her hand sliding beneath the table to still his, their eyes locked in a smoldering standoff. "I make people who do, pay for their bad behavior."

"Really?" Constantine asked, with clear interest in his tone. "A real good girl, are you?" He nudged her legs a bit farther apart and then maneuvered their hands so that hers settled on top of her core. His forehead settled against hers and he said softly, "You aren't acting like such a good girl right now, Nicole."

The way he said her name—with a roll of the *L*—made her hot. She couldn't answer him, biting her lip to hold back a moan, as their combined fingers brushed along the tiny silk barrier of her panties. His lips brushed her ear as he murmured something in Spanish that she didn't understand. Then he said, "I like a woman who knows when to take charge," and his fingers worked with hers to shove aside the panties and brush her swollen clit. "A woman who knows how to get results."

Her lashes fluttered, her mind lost in her body's demands. Her fingers worked with his, sliding along the slick folds of her core, gently caressing. Teasing. When Constantine inserted one long finger inside her body, she could barely breathe for the pleasure. He cupped her mound with both their hands, massaging even as he stroked her inner wall.

"Come for me, baby. You're so wet. I know you want to come."

He got that right. She was barely containing her desire to rock with the motion of his hand, or rather *their* hands. "I…I…oh…"

She fought a moan that would surely draw unwanted attention. But it just felt so…good. She couldn't hold back. She needed this, needed release so badly.

As if Constantine knew what she struggled with, his mouth covered hers, swallowing the sound of gratification before it filled the room. It was a kiss that branded her with sensual heat, his tongue delivering such perfection it seemed to stroke her clit just as his thumb did.

Nicole quivered with the impact, her body tensing with the onset of release—a release that became so intense, she hurt with the pleasure of it. He worked her through the orgasm, his fingers, tongue and hand taking her higher and higher…then bringing her to slow, sweet bliss.

When eventually Nicole stilled, Constantine's fingers remained between her legs, and she knew she should be embarrassed. Instead, she stared up at him, dumbfounded by how lost she'd become in this man, this stranger. How easily he'd made her forget her surroundings. Forget her life. Forget the past and even the present.

Nicole had delved into some fairly kinky, and quite agreeable, places with her ex. But never, ever had she felt removed from the world. Never had she just experienced the pleasure as an escape. Always before, she'd felt…detached—like a spectator who watched from outside the scene.

This was new territory, and Nicole didn't even know how to react.

Constantine eased her clothes back into place and then smoothed her hair down, his touch gentle, his expression unreadable. Maybe even a bit dark. He drew a deep breath, and then squeezed his eyes shut. One second. Two.

His lashes lifted. "I'm sorry."

"For what?" she asked, confused.

"I have to go," he said, and without another word, he popped out of the seat and left.

Nicole stared after him, stunned.

Had he really just gotten up and left? Simply given her an orgasm and then said goodbye?

CONSTANTINE STRADDLED his motorcycle and kick-started the engine, beyond ready to feel the bike's speed beneath him. He'd been a fool to take things so far with Nicole, not walking away the minute he'd ruled out foul play from her agenda. But no. He'd stayed. Drawn into her presence, into his attraction to the woman, he'd stayed.

For some crazy reason, he couldn't help himself. Seeing her so hot for him, so eager to be pleased, had driven him to the edge.

"Chingado," he cursed, and added a few other Spanish adjectives under his breath.

He'd done what he had to, Constantine told himself, trying to feel better about his actions. Survival demanded desperate moves. Surely, she'd understand. Nicole had studied the Alvarez case. She knew how vicious, even poisonous, the man could be.

Shaking his head, Constantine laughed, but without humor. Who was he fooling? He'd stayed because he'd wanted Nicole. Wanted her damn bad.

Even now, he could halfway convince himself to go back inside that hotel, get a room and fuck her all night long. Why not? The damage was done. She'd hate him when she found out he was her new star witness against Alvarez.

He muttered again, and revved his engine, forcing himself to drive away. Hating what this job had turned him into, and vowing to walk away when this was over.

Nobody could gamble as much as he had without it catching up with him and he knew it.

3

"YOU HAVE TO USE his testimony. This man, this *agent,* has spent three years of his life undercover for this. He gave up everything to see Alvarez fall."

"I don't have to do anything," Nicole insisted, flattening her palms on her desk, and leveling Agent Flores with a stare. "It's two days before the trial, and you're telling me I can't even meet this witness before he goes on the stand. That's insane." She leaned back in her well-worn chair, the overused metal base squeaking. "I'm a lot of things, Agent Flores, but crazy isn't one of them." *Unless you count how I acted in that bar over the past weekend,* she added silently.

He eased to the edge of his chair, where he sat directly across from her. They'd been arguing a good fifteen minutes. He'd been on his feet and back down again more times than a pogo stick.

"I told you," he said, through gritted teeth, "it has been a delicate operation and though I am the lead on this, everyone on the task force agreed we should wait until the last minute. The longer Agent Vega is inside, the less time he's a target, and the more time we have to gather evidence."

His explanation didn't please her and sarcasm laced

her reply. "Glad you and your task force are in agreement. Might have been nice if you'd included our office."

His cell phone rang, and he reached into his suit jacket and withdrew it. "I need to take this."

Nicole nodded in understanding, glad for a momentary reprieve. Agent Flores seemed determined, pressing her hard on this witness. A tiny spot of concern flared at his absolute insistence. She'd been given second chair on this case, but her boss, Dean, the U.S. Attorney over Western Texas, had a wife with cancer, and he had all but handed her the first-chair duty. He was counting on her not to screw up, and she didn't want to let him down. And though she knew dismissing a material witness with critical information was a bad idea, she couldn't feel good about blindly trusting a person's credibility.

Easing back in her chair, used by numerous others before her time, she glanced around the room, taking in the corkboard bulletin board and steel file cabinets.

Her office wasn't fancy. Her job wasn't, either. Lousy pay. Long hours. Lots of yelling when things went wrong. Nicole wouldn't change a thing. She'd seen the other side of things, the money and power. And she'd paid the price.

Agent Flores, thankfully, put away his phone. Nicole was ready to end this conversation. "You can't bring a witness in from nowhere and expect me to be okay with it." She held up a staying finger to stop the argument she knew he'd offer. "We are talking about putting the biggest drug lord in the known world behind bars. I'm *not* going to do anything to jeopardize that. I haven't even met your witness."

"The agent is your ticket to conviction. If you can't see that, maybe the U.S. Attorney can."

That flared her temper. She didn't want Dean bothered with this. He had enough to deal with right now. "Don't even go there, because I promise, you won't like the results. Dean doesn't like it when his people are crossed. He'll back me and shut you down. The bottom line is this—we won't put a witness on the stand who we can't meet before the trial. Either give me a meeting with your agent or this discussion is over."

"It's too dangerous," he said, his lips tight, his words terse.

"Dangerous is going into court blind," she said, pushing to her feet, a strand of blond hair slipping from her neat bun to fall into her eyes. Swiping at it, she started gathering her things for court and shoving them into her briefcase. She wasn't foolish enough to walk away from a witness that could help her case; she just needed to validate his worth, which meant playing hardball. "I have to go."

He stared at her, silent a little too long. "You need him, Nicole." His voice was low. Intense.

She knew Agent Flores quite well. He rarely used her first name, and she didn't miss the plea being issued. Nicole felt torn about her decision, questioning her own judgment when she normally would not. She imagined she had her weekend adventure in that bar to thank for that.

She hadn't used her head then. And she didn't want to let Alvarez slip away by refusing a witness. Still, gambling on an erotic encounter with a stranger was one thing. This case was too important to roll the dice and take unnecessary risks. Her resolve thickened. Putting a witness on the stand under these circumstances would be reckless, and she had no doubt that her boss would agree.

"I can't give in on this," she repeated. "There's simply too much at stake."

"Fine," he said, drawing a deep breath and letting it out. "You can meet him."

She rearranged some of the things on her desk. "I'm listening."

"I have to talk to Vega, but he won't come here, I know that much. You'll have to go to him."

That didn't sound good, but neither did missing out on a chance to ensure a conviction. "Where?"

"I'll call you with the details," he said. "But tonight. I'll make it happen. For you alone, though. No one else. Vega is going to be pissed as it is."

"You won't be able to reach me. I won't be out of court until around six."

He nodded. "Call me when you're leaving. I'll have everything arranged by then. And don't tell anyone else about this. It's too dangerous. Any leak could get him killed."

"I know the way it works," she said, but a feeling of unease danced along her nerve endings. Nicole grabbed her briefcase and purse and headed for the door, but not before fixing him with a hard stare. "Don't make me regret this."

NICOLE SAT IN the passenger's side of a government-issued, unmarked Buick Sedan with an unfriendly U.S. Marshal driving. She stared out of the window, noting the sun shrinking beyond the horizon as a rainbow of color filled the sky. She'd been required to stop at three pay phones and then leave her own vehicle behind. Why she had allowed herself to be talked into coming out to the middle of nowhere, she didn't know.

As soon as she asked the question, though, she knew the answer.

Alvarez.

He was as bad as they came, linked directly and indirectly to getting a lot of kids hooked on drugs. To Nicole, the kids mattered in a big way. She'd grown up in Padre, ten minutes from Brownsville, a city on the border of Mexico. A city that sucked teens into drugs, both using and dealing. She'd seen them destroy too many people.

She was about to ask how much farther they had to go, when she spotted a small house tucked away in a cluster of trees, nearly invisible but for the moonlight.

As they drew nearer, she could see it was more a cabin than a house. Vehicles parked in front were further confirmation she was at the right place. Rather old, the cabin had a rusty tin roof and boards hanging off the porch.

The marshal pulled up next to a truck and killed the ignition. She started to reach for her briefcase, but before she could turn, the door was jerked open.

Shocked, she whirled toward the door to find a stranger there, another marshal she assumed. "What—" Her words were cut off by the harsh look on the man's face.

"Get out."

One glance at the driver's seat told of the other marshal's exit. She eyed the gruff man at her door. "I just need to gather my things." Nicole paused. "My briefcase and purse." Something made her hesitate, waiting for a reply.

Perhaps his size. The man was a monster. Bigger than big, with linebacker-wide shoulders, he had a menacing edge to his presence. A jagged-edged scar decorated his right cheek, making him seem even more sinister. She couldn't help but wonder how he got it.

"First, you meet Vega." It was an order. "If he trusts you, then I'll get your stuff."

If *he* trusted *her?* Hello? She was the one here to decide if *she* trusted him. She opened her mouth to say so, but then quickly shut it. Something about this guy said, don't argue.

"Let's go," he said, sounding like a guard talking to his prisoner. He reached for her as if he might grab her arm.

Appalled, she jerked her shoulder away and glared. "Don't you dare touch me."

Defiance flashed in his eyes, but for only a mere second, before it disappeared behind an indecipherable mask. Taking a step backward, he gave her a gallant wave forward. "Ladies first."

Mumbling a few, barely audible, choice words, she stepped out of the car. Tossing her hair over her shoulder with an angry flip of the wrist, she marched ahead, wishing she'd left it pulled back. Her nerves were frazzled and her professional armor, which included her normal hairdo, would be welcome right about now.

Two men stood outside the door of the cabin, guarding the entryway, and blocking her passage forward. She glanced at the man on the left, noting his sunbaked skin and short brown hair. His counterpart to the right was his exact opposite in appearance. Fair hair and skin, and shoulder-length, tangled hair, which gave him a wild look. Neither looked friendly.

They both seemed as cranky as the man on her heels. "Great," she mumbled, as she started up the porch steps. "They come in threes."

As she stepped toward the men, neither moved. She'd changed into sensible dress pants and boots, but she still sported heels. Man, would she like to dig one of them into a foot to get a reaction. She'd never been treated this way before, and she planned to vocalize as much later.

Apparently, she had the green light to enter the house by herself. She looked from one man to the other. "You mean I don't need my hand held?"

The sunbaked guard dog answered. "He knows you're here."

She didn't ask how. Didn't want to know. She just wanted to get this entire affair over with.

Without another word, Nicole reached for the doorknob. The hinges creaked as she pushed it open, almost as if it were issuing a warning to the occupant of the house.

"Hello?" she called out as she continued through a narrow entranceway.

No answer.

Inside, she found herself in what appeared to be a living room. She took in her surroundings quickly, noting the rustic, sparse furnishings. A couch, a chair and one table were the extent of the décor. There were no pictures, no knickknacks that people collect and display as they go through life. Nothing.

Either no one actually lived in the house, or the inhabitants cared little for life, in general. Probably, no one lived here. After all, it was some sort of safe house.

As her inspection continued, her gaze moved to a huge rock fireplace, the centerpiece of the room. A weird feeling made her stomach flutter. Her gaze shifted, as if instinctively, to a corner window.

That's when she saw him. This man called Vega.

She could hardly believe she hadn't noticed him before. It wasn't as if the room were huge or the man small. Somehow, he blended or hid or something, whatever it was, to make himself invisible. He was so still, so utterly unmoving, that it was as if he were a part of the room.

His back was to her, but she knew with complete certainty that he was one hundred percent aware of her every move. He faced the window, seeming to survey the view beyond the glass.

Her stomach flip-flopped as the feeling that had drawn her gaze seemed to intensify. A carnal awareness slid through her body, her skin heating, her heart thumping like a drum in her chest.

She knew him.

No.

It couldn't be.

She swallowed, finding it hard to process mentally what her physical self was telling her. How could the stranger from the bar be here?

But it *was* him. She knew it with every fiber of her being.

If he were here now, and he had also been at the bar… A sick flutter went through her stomach as the possibilities flew through her mind. A combination of anger and embarrassment began to churn in her gut, and she shoved the worthless emotions aside as premature. Maybe it wasn't him, the man from the bar. Maybe her mind was playing tricks on her. She studied the man from behind, hoping it wasn't Constantine. Praying she'd not been betrayed, sucked into a trap by someone using her desire as a weapon. The very thing that had destroyed her life once before.

Then, as if answering her silent question, he turned, giving her a view of the true man. Their eyes locked and held. Recognition came to her mind, confirming what her body and senses already knew. This *was* the man from the bar.

Images of Friday night, of how he'd touched her, played in her mind. She saw it in his eyes, too. The memories. Maybe a flash of guilt. The knowledge that he'd taken from her without being honest.

He gave her a quick nod. "Hello, Nicole."

The way he said her name, with that sexy Spanish accent, sent a shiver down her spine. And she hated him for having that impact on her. No. She hated herself for allowing this stranger to deceive her. For being weak enough to become prey to a man with an agenda.

"That's my name," she said, stiffening. "What's yours? Constantine? Vega? Where do the lies start and stop?"

He leaned against the wall, crossing one booted foot over the other. Soft denim hugged his muscular thighs, drawing her gaze and making her remember touching him.

Being touched by him.

Though he made no effort to close the distance between them on a physical level, his eyes seemed to touch her more intimately.

Her fists balled at her sides as she fought the urge to launch herself at him and smack his face, to make him pay for what he'd taken from her—her control, her self-respect.

She drew in a slow breath, cautiously concealing her discomfort behind an unreadable mask reserved for prosecuting in a courtroom. This man had only gotten where he had with her because she'd let him. He wouldn't get past her guard again.

"Well?" she demanded.

He studied her for several seconds, his gaze far too probing for Nicole's comfort. She felt as if he knew her secrets, and she wondered if he did. Just how much of her life had he investigated before he'd seduced her?

"Constantine," he then said, confirming his name. At least one thing about that night had been true. "Agent Constantine Vega." He paused as if giving her time to digest his words. "I can give you the conviction you seek, Ms. Ward."

A conviction and an orgasm, she thought bitterly. How perfectly efficient of him. And devious. He'd been after something. What? Her eyes narrowed on him, suspicion replacing her anger. Agent Flores had given no indication that he knew she'd met Agent Vega before today. If he didn't know, then Vega had been acting on his own. Agent Flores trusted this man, which lent some support to his credibility. Still…could either or both of them be working for Alvarez? Had she been seduced by the enemy?

"You know what," Nicole said, starting to back away. "This was a bad idea." She turned and headed for the door. She managed all of three steps when she found herself whirled around, pulled tight against a long, hard body. Her breath lodged in her throat, fear and arousal merging together, radiating through her limbs. Her hands pressed against his chest, her legs and hips aligned with his.

"Let me go," she whispered hoarsely, wishing like hell she didn't still want him, wondering why she did when he'd used her in such a way, and when she knew she couldn't believe whatever he said.

"Not until you hear me out," he countered in a low, dangerous voice. "I'm no angel, but I'm not the enemy. I had no option but to check you out before I came forward. I trust my instincts, not a file folder with your name and stats inside. Until I knew I had a sense of who you are, I wasn't going to come forward." That pissed her off and some of her fear slid away.

"How exactly did sticking your hand up my skirt convince you I could be trusted?" An icy tone chilled her words.

"What happened between us wasn't supposed to. I didn't plan to want you, nor did I plan for you to want me. Am I sorry? I should be, but I'm not. My only regret is walking away before we'd finished what we started. But *this* moment was destined to come anyway."

Call him on his boldness, Nicole told herself, *and demand an apology.* That is what *she* should do. Just as she should be indignant, appalled. Instead, Nicole found herself savoring his seductive claim of a shared secret, remembering the bliss of his hands caressing her skin, seducing her until she was ready to melt. Upset at herself over the way he'd tricked her, she reached for that ripe anger, still burning inside her, and let it expand in her chest. The man was leading her down a passion-filled path to trouble, awakening a dangerously erotic part of her that had once ruled her life. She should walk away. But she couldn't. Not with so much on the line. Not when Constantine might really be the key to Alvarez's conviction.

"I'll hear what you have to say," she said, because it was her only option. "On one condition." Constantine arched a brow in silent question. She shoved at his chest. "Let go of me and do not touch me again."

Her body might still remember the pleasure he'd delivered, but she wasn't a fool. This man was trouble. And now he'd had the audacity to use that big body of his to force her to listen. She didn't like it. It was time he learned he wasn't in charge anymore. No seductive prowess was going to change that, either, she vowed.

4

NICOLE GOT TO HIM in a big way—a way no woman had done in far too long to remember. So much so, that her anger challenged him, made him want to kiss her into submission.

Let her go or kiss her? A tough call. Her lips were full and red—tempting lips that he already knew tasted sinfully sweet. Yes, kissing her would be a delicious distraction from the hell he called his life right now. But then, it wouldn't work toward earning her trust, nor would it aid his efforts to put Alvarez into permanent retirement.

Constantine ground his teeth together, accepting the inevitable conclusion that he must behave. He gave her lips one last wistful look before forcing himself to release her and step backward.

Nicole immediately crossed her arms in front of her body in a guarded stance. The act thrust her breasts high, giving his eyes yet another delicious distraction. Damn, the woman was killing him.

He sat down on the arm of the couch, which served dual purposes. It put Nicole out of reach and brought the two of them closer to eye level, so he wouldn't tower over her. The goal was trust, not intimidation.

Their gazes connected, silent tension filling the air.

She was angry and probably embarrassed, though he doubted she would admit that part. "I think you should know," he said, attempting a path to a truce, "no one knew I was following you, nor do they know about what happened between us."

"How long, exactly, were you following me?" she asked, her boot doing a slow tap on the floor, telling of her agitation as much as the steely look in her beautiful eyes.

Inwardly, he cringed before he answered. "Two days." He left out how much he'd enjoyed watching her those two days, how many ways he'd fantasized about making love to her. He figured it wouldn't help his situation any.

She made a frustrated sound; her hands dropped to her sides—perfectly manicured hands with pink nails curling into her palms. "Two days." The words were flat, her cheeks flushed. Her gaze dropped to the floor as she mumbled, "Two days and I never suspected a thing." It wasn't a question. It was more a statement of disbelief directed at herself. Her chin lifted, eyes latching on to his with accusation. "You expect me to believe the feds let you disappear for two days without any idea where you were?"

"I wasn't supposed to pull out of Alvarez's operation until the last minute. It left me less risk of exposure. But three years of my life were on the line, and I know how easily Alvarez corrupts people. I didn't care what your file said. I needed to get a sense of who you were myself. Alvarez is going to find someone in the middle of this to corrupt, I promise you, if he hasn't already."

"I know Alvarez's type," she quickly asserted.

"Sweetheart, you only think you know his type." Constantine had seen things—hell, done things himself during these past few years—that would bring grown men to their knees. "Murder is worthy of popcorn and a soda to Alvarez. As for corrupting someone inside this case, he'll do whatever it takes to get out of that jail cell. Even threaten the lives of their families." His voice softened. "I approached you that night as a means of survival. What happened from there was pure chemistry."

Her lips thinned. She opened her mouth to speak and then closed it again. "I need my briefcase from the car. There are questions—" A slight sound on the roof sent her gaze upward and Constantine to his feet. "You heard that, too, right?" she asked, worry etching in her lovely face.

He had heard all right. Which was why his hand now rested on his side, ready to draw his Glock. "Most likely the wind," he stated, but it wasn't. He'd grown up here and he knew every sound, every nuance.

Two knocks sounded on the front door, a code for his men before entry. A marshal known as Smith entered, his big body tense, his expression grim. Constantine cursed under his breath, knowing the news was bad before it was even spoken. "We have company," Smith stated, confirming Constantine's assumption.

"What does that mean?" Nicole asked.

Drawing his gun from the holster on his shoulder, Constantine ignored her question, focusing on getting the facts. "How many?"

"I wish I knew," Smith said, no longer hiding his weapon. It was in his hand, ready to be put to use. "We have movement on the roof. Two spotted coming up the west side of the property by foot. Probably more we have yet to identify."

"Oh, my God," Nicole whispered. "I did everything Agent Flores told me to do."

And Flores had tailed her to make sure she wasn't followed. Someone had betrayed him, not that Constantine found this surprising. That's why he had an escape plan plotted. And even that was only partially shared with Agent Flores, who he trusted as well as he trusted anyone. Truth was, he trusted no one completely. Not after everything he'd seen these past three years. If he got her to the woods, he could get her to safety.

He turned to Nicole, hands going to her shoulders; he fixed her in a steady stare. "How they found us doesn't matter. What matters is our safety. And as you've already seen, I don't take chances. I plan in advance. I can get us out of here."

She seemed to be weighing his words, then said, "I know how to fire a gun."

"Why doesn't that surprise me?" he said, thinking that not much about this woman did. He bent down, removing a lightweight Wesson 35 from a holster around his ankle and handing it to her. "Six rounds, one in the chamber. Got it?"

She nodded. "Yeah. I got it. I wish I didn't have to, but I do."

Constantine wished the same thing, but he had to admire her courage. No tears for this one.

He turned to Smith and told him, "Cover the east side of the cabin so we make it the woods." He grabbed Nicole's hand and pulled her toward the kitchen window.

"What if they're right outside?" Nicole demanded as he opened the glass.

"Smith and his men will cover us," he assured her.

"The same ones that made sure no one found us?"

He hiked himself up on the counter. She had a point,

but he didn't say that. "I'll go first so I can make sure it's safe." His fingers brushed her cheek. "Don't fret. No one knows these woods like I do. I grew up here." He let his hand drop. "And I put up with three years of Alvarez's shit. I have no intention of either of us dying before we make that sorry bastard feel some pain." Then, he lowered his voice, his words full of promise. "Trust me."

ON THE RUN, the very man who had betrayed her the week before now held her hand, leading her through the wilderness—her lifeline from those who hunted them. And on the run they were. For hours it seemed. They'd run and run some more.

Long ago, Constantine had broken off the heels on her boots, but not before painful blisters had formed on her toes. Still, she wasn't complaining. They'd had a close call with a couple of Alvarez's men near the cabin, barely ducking out of sight. That was enough to make Nicole thankful to be alive—blisters be damned. Right now, she had only one thing on her mind, and that was staying alive.

Constantine drew abruptly to a halt, pulling her to a squatting position behind a cluster of bushes. Nicole obliged, struggling to catch her breath, the humidity making the air thick and hard to inhale. Her hair clung to her neck, sticky and uncomfortable. There was no wind, so the heat was a stifling wall of discomfort. Thunder rolled in the distance, warning of rain, and right now, she welcomed the relief it would bring.

With a silent look, Constantine let her know his intentions—he was going to scout ahead as he had several times before. She barely inclined her head and he was gone, moving with a silent, stealthlike agility that a man his size shouldn't possess. But then, he'd stayed alive inside Alvarez's gang. No doubt, that had to have taken some fancy footwork. Three years of living that life was a long time. That he had a backup plan, a hideout no one knew about, shouldn't surprise her. She imagined those three years had made him resourceful.

Alone now behind the cluster of bushes, she peered into the darkness, searching for trouble, her ears straining for any sound that might signal danger. Nicole sucked in a surprised breath as Constantine was suddenly behind her, no sound warning of his approach. Every time he touched her, awareness teased her nerve endings, taunting her with her inability to control its presence. She rotated around to face him, her thigh aligned with his, pressed close. Their eyes locked, the connection hitting her with lightning force, attraction sizzling around them despite the danger they faced.

But there was more than attraction that lured Nicole to Constantine at present. Crazy as it was, this stranger, a man who'd lied to her only a week before, offered comfort and security that she desperately needed right now.

"Not much farther," he murmured, his voice a low whisper.

"Shouldn't we call someone?" she asked, matching his low tone, wishing she hadn't left her cell phone back at the cabin.

"No need. A rendezvous is set up with Flores in the event I run into trouble. A time and location not far from here. We just need to get underground and safe until then. Besides, we don't know who we can trust, and any call could be monitored."

"If I don't show up tomorrow, they might do something crazy to delay the trial. I know you don't want that."

"What I want is to stay alive." He pushed to his feet, staring down at her as he offered her his hand.

Nicole took a moment to stare up at the foreboding, but oh-so-sexy male, before slipping her palm into his. His cheeks were chiseled, his jaw strong, something in those dark eyes wary and lonely. He was a stranger who'd snuck past her guard in far too many ways, an undercover agent who oozed danger and sex, with no telling what kind of sordid past. Yet in just a week's time, she'd put both her life, and her libido, in his hands.

Hands she hoped were as experienced at surviving in the wild as they were at giving pleasure.

5

RAIN FELL SLOWLY, steadily, and seeped into Nicole's clothes and cooled her skin as she followed Constantine through a heavily wooded area. Tree branches and bushes had to be shoved aside and dodged. For a stormy night, the sky was remarkably bright, the way a sky was lit before a tornado. Nicole didn't want to think about that now. She focused on keeping pace with Constantine, pushing herself as hard as she could. That was until her foot hit a rock that bit through a sore spot on her sole. Pain rocketed up her shin, and to her complete dismay, her ankle twisted to the side.

Constantine grabbed her arm to steady her. Suddenly the deadly sound of a rattlesnake filled the air. "Don't move, *cariña,*" he warned, his voice low, tight. "Don't move."

"Oh, God," she whispered hoarsely, fear shooting adrenaline through her body and telling her to run. Somehow she stayed still. "Where is it?"

But he didn't respond with words. With agility and speed, Constantine somehow pulled his gun and fired. Her body stiffened, ready for the snake's strike if he missed.

Instead, she found herself engulfed in his strong

arms, his hand sliding down the back of her head. "It's over. It's dead."

Nicole blinked up at him as the words sank in, and then she abruptly whirled around to see the proof. Constantine shined his penlight so she could see the snake. She breathed calmly at the sight of the dead rattler, but it didn't last, as his arms dropped away and he grabbed her hand, and told her, "We need to *move*. That gunshot just announced our location." He had no sooner spoken the words than he tugged her into motion.

Her heart pounded in her ears; her adrenaline, still high from her snake encounter, now shot beyond her control. Constantine was relentless in the path before him, half dragging her, clearly compelled to get distance between them and where the gunshot had sounded.

Several branches snapped to their right, and Constantine stilled instantly, pulling Nicole down into the bushes. Nicole's stomach churned. Oh, no. They'd been found.

Constantine motioned to other bushes that formed a circle and pulled her into its center. There was barely room for the two of them. Next, he retrieved the Wesson revolver again from his boot holster, where it had been secured while they were on the run. He pressed it into her palm and then slid his cheek against hers, his lips to her ear. "This is about staying alive. Don't talk yourself out of pulling the trigger." Leaning back, he searched her face, showing his in the process. A chill raced down her spine. Those warm, chocolate-brown eyes of his held fiery determination and strength; she could see he was willing to demand the same of her but he didn't have to. She'd do anything to protect herself. She drew a breath and nodded her understanding. Satisfaction filled his gaze.

He leaned close again, the warmth of his body penetrating her wet skin, the stubble of his chin brushing her cheek with an intimate touch. "Don't come out until I say to."

The contact disappeared as quickly as it had come, leaving Nicole with a fluttering heart. Constantine shifted his weight, poised to dart away, then male voices sounded nearby—one she recognized.

Nicole grabbed his arm, relief flooding her. She whispered, "That's David Wright. He's an FBI agent. A good one." They were saved. She started to move, ready to get the heck out of the woods. About to stand, she quickly found herself yanked downward. Suddenly, her back was molded to Constantine's chest, his chin on her shoulder, lips next to her ear. "Trust no one," he warned. "No one."

Irritated at being manhandled, she half hissed her low reply. "I know him. He's honest."

"You can't know that. Not with Alvarez involved."

"I do," she insisted. Her instincts were rarely wrong, and they'd served her well in her job.

"And if his family is threatened, then what? Would he protect you over them?" He didn't give her time to respond. "Choose now. Trust me or trust David. But if you go to David, go with your gun drawn because you're going to need it."

He let go of her with such abruptness, she barely steadied herself from tumbling over. She maneuvered around to face him, and the look he fixed on her was hard with steely anger.

Time seemed to stand still, just as it often did in the courtroom when she found herself under fire, when she was forced to make an educated gamble. She had to roll the dice here, and her money was on Constantine.

Her chest was tight with conflicting emotion, but her decision was made. She settled back down on her heels, planting herself, silently telling him she was staying. The voices were coming closer. Out of her peripheral vision, she realized Constantine had drawn his weapon and was aiming it through the cover of the bushes. She followed his lead and did the same.

"Damn it. Where the hell are they?" It was David. He was close enough that Nicole could see his face through the branches.

"Relax," the other man said. "The gunshot puts them within reach. If they aren't already dead, we'll make sure they get that way."

"Relax?" David's voice was filled with disbelief. "My wife, my children…everyone I care about has been threatened."

"Alvarez gets what he wants no matter what it takes. You should have taken the money he offered you and run. I did."

Nicole felt as if she'd been punched in the stomach. It wasn't news that someone like Alvarez would stoop so low, but the magnitude of his reach was downright chilling. If she wanted to stay on this case—and all this experience did was make her more determined to put the brakes on Alvarez—she would have to go underground until the trial. And she would have to do so with Constantine. The one person she knew she could trust to help her stay alive. She slowly inhaled. A man who was dangerous to her for reasons that had nothing to do with this case.

David and the other man exchanged a few more words before splitting up. For long minutes, neither she nor Constantine moved. He was like a statue—completely, utterly still, yet somehow alert, ready.

Abruptly he pushed to his feet and stared down at her, his expression hard, his anger toward her obvious. "Let's move." And he took off walking. This time there was no offer of his hand. He was pissed.

Nicole watched in disbelief as he pushed through the bushes and walked away. How could he be pissed? She had every right to doubt him, every reason. He turned back to her, and glowered. "Now." His voice was low, but, oh-so-lethal.

She glowered at him and then did what she had to do—marched forward. What choice did she have? Right now, he had the upper hand. She needed his ability to survive against Alvarez and his thugs. She'd gain back some control though—somehow. This was about more than surviving this night.

She didn't want to die, but then, she didn't want to lose Alvarez, or even the careful confines of structure she'd put around her world. Not now, not ever. And certainly not because of some hot Latino man with attitude who thought he could steal her orgasm under false pretenses as if he had every right as long as he cloaked it in work-related precautions. Well, he hadn't the right. And they hadn't fully explored that topic yet, but they would. Oh, yes, they would.

HEAVY RAIN TORTURED them for a good hour until minutes before they arrived at their destination. He turned to Nicole then, the first time he had even considered speaking to her since their clash over trust. His acute irritation was irrational but no less real. So real it had driven him to be a coldhearted ass, pushing Nicole harder than he should have, ignoring the pain he knew those damn boots were causing her, communicating nothing. But the simple truth was, he wanted her to give him her trust without question. Hell, he wanted more than her trust—he wanted her.

"This is it," Constantine informed Nicole, inspecting the cave entrance a few feet away, a cave he had explored with his father as a young boy.

The minute he'd registered the way her wet clothes clung to her curves, he ground his teeth. He wasn't a man without control, and he'd certainly known his share of pleasure, his share of women—some so beautiful, they could bring a man to his knees. They hadn't gotten to him though, that was the thing. But Nicole just might have that power, and he wasn't sure he liked it.

He found himself lost in an inspection of Nicole, trying to decide why she drove him so insane with desire. Water clung to her lashes, to her lips, her hair soaked to the sides of her face, emphasizing her high cheekbones and full mouth. He followed the path of rain as it dotted her face, her neck, her blouse outlining her full breasts and erect nipples. His cock twitched, and he bit back a growl. He needed to focus on business, not desire. He should bed this woman and get her out of his system. Starting something he hadn't finished was where he'd gone wrong. That was it. That was what was killing him. Get her naked and beneath him so he could stop fantasizing about it.

The decision made, he savored those plump, pert breasts a moment longer, before his gaze lifted. Their eyes locked, collided actually, in a fiery contact that took his twitch to a full hard-on. Damn it, distraction was dangerous. She was that and more at this point.

"When we go inside the cave, it'll be pitch-black. Just hang by the wall while I open the door to the hideout. There is light, food and supplies there. We have a few hours before our rendezvous with Flores."

Her face went instantly pale. "Are we talking about *hiding* in that cave?"

His brows dipped. "Right. There's a hidden cavern beneath the surface. Even if they search the cave, they won't find us."

"That's, ah…" She hesitated. "I guess I didn't mention I'm claustrophobic?"

Once he managed to maneuver her inside the cave, he kept her near enough to the entrance that darkness didn't completely consume her, giving her time to adjust to the small space.

He pressed her against the wall. "Don't move. I'll be right back."

She grabbed his wrist, and tightly wrapped one leg around his calf. "Where are you going?" Her voice held panic.

Crap. The woman was killing him. He wanted nothing more than to have those long legs wrapped tight around him, but now wasn't the time. He was about to say as much when he realized she was shaking. The tough-as-nails prosecutor, who'd barely blinked when faced with guns and a snake, was quaking in her boots over a phobia. Her fear was as irrational as his anger over her mistrust, but that didn't matter. In fact, somehow it made her seem more human, more vulnerable. The tough courtroom persona that she often showed had fled completely.

Everything inside him went soft in a way he didn't know he was still capable of. The past few years had made him hard, not easily enticed into sympathy. Just another bit of proof this woman had bewitched him in a big way.

"Easy, *cariña*," he whispered, his thumbs stroking her cheeks. Her face was in shadow, but he didn't have to see it to know the fear it held. He could feel it in the way she clung to him, in the ragged way she was breathing. "I haven't let anything happen to you thus far, and I'm not now."

She seemed to struggle with words, her expression tormented. "When I was a kid, I went exploring a vacant apartment complex near my house. I fell through a floor and was trapped for hours under some boards. I've…never been able to kick the trapped thing. It's stupid, but—"

His thumb brushed her lips, silencing the words. "It's not stupid," he said, sensing this wasn't a confession she delivered with ease. His chest tightened with that knowledge, with unexplainable emotion that he didn't want to feel. "You could have died. But you didn't and you're not going to now. I used to come here when I was a kid, actually. With my father. I've spent lots of time in this cave."

Her hands went to his wrists as if she were afraid he was about to leave. "You're sure it's safe?"

"Very. And we'll only be here a few hours before we make our connection with Flores. Give it a try." He paused intentionally, careful not to push too hard. "Yes?"

She hesitated again, and then said, "Okay." The one word quivered with discernible apprehension. He was proud of her for the bravery it took to speak it. Phobias were like criminals lurking in the mind waiting to attack, and were hard, often impossible, to defeat. He was lucky that some of the things he'd seen hadn't done the same to him. Some of his fellow agents hadn't been as fortunate.

"Good," he said of her agreement, reaching behind him to ease her leg from his with gentle insistence. "Stay here. I'll be right back." He settled her foot back on the ground and worked her fingers from his wrists.

He realized then that he'd gotten the trust he wanted. But now that he had it, that trust felt like a hot potato he should toss back. All the women he'd been with these past three years were of Alvarez's world. They were criminals, no better than the man they served, because of their choices. He'd tried to group Nicole into that category—just part of his assignment, gratifying his own needs. But Nicole wasn't one of those other women; she wasn't anything like them.

At the same time, he himself wasn't the type of man who walked in *her* world. He barely remembered his real name half the time. He didn't even have a home right now. Everything was in storage. His life was danger, sex, poison, in all different flavors. Nicole's world was a direct contrast to his: full of order and the pursuit of justice, by way of perfect appearances and rules.

Yet…he still wanted her. Not only did he want her, he had to have her. Just one time, he told himself. He'd make sure she enjoyed every last minute of it, too.

6

NICOLE HATED DEFEAT, and defeat created by one's own self was the worst kind. For all the structure and control in her life, claustrophobia had been her nemesis. She'd learned relaxation techniques to deal with it. She had even managed to get on a plane, albeit slightly sedated, but still, she'd managed to fly and not panic. She could do the same with this damn cave, and doing it without drugs would be a sign of real progress.

Easier said than done, she thought, as she stared at the black hole Constantine had disappeared into, and waited impatiently for the light he'd promised. All sorts of horrid fates that could befall him raced through her mind. Maybe a wild animal? Another snake?

Her eyes went to the giant rock Constantine had removed from blocking the hole that seemed barely big enough for him to slide down into. Retrieving a rope hidden somewhere inside the cave, he'd tied it around the rock, which she assumed was to pull it back in place when ready. She couldn't see how else the rock would get there once they were belowground. Quite ingenious.

Suddenly, a warm glow filled the cavern, and Nicole let out a breath she hadn't even realized she'd been holding. That was the signal to follow him. She steadied herself, pressing one balled hand to the center of her chest and her racing heart. She could do this, and she would not hyperventilate. Inhale, exhale. Okay. Maybe this was just what she needed. To face her fear.

Thunder crashed overhead, almost directly on top of her, and Nicole jumped at the ferocious sound. The violence of the storm somehow reminded her of the violence hunting them. This stupid phobia was not going to get her killed.

She didn't give herself time to think any further; she quickly narrowed her gaze on the makeshift stairs Constantine had told her about. Clear on where to step, she went into action, and started down the wall, the steel stakes, thankfully, as sturdy as Constantine had promised. She passed an electric lantern—the kind that campers use—hanging to her left a few steps down. It was a comforting sight as these lanterns weren't likely to burn out.

She focused on each step, refusing to look down, except that she ran out of metal stakes too quickly, with nowhere to go, and the ground still a long ways off. Nicole twisted around, placing her back to the wall, to find Constantine standing directly below her. She scanned the area, surprised to find it the size of a small bedroom.

Constantine held his hands out. "Jump," he said, pulling her attention to him. "I'll catch you."

If she tried, Nicole knew she could think of a million reasons not to jump. But then, she didn't want to try. She was frustrated with herself—for her fear, her blisters, for letting herself expose a weakness to a mere stranger. She jumped, her heart all but stopping with the act.

A second later, Constantine's hands settled on her hips, the fingers of one hand spread on her backside, seemingly holding her without effort. The heart that had stuttered was now back to pounding a rapid drumroll.

Constantine slid her body down his rock-hard perfect one with delicious slowness, their hips melting together. Somehow they froze like that, her feet not yet on the ground. The instant her gaze found the heat in his, her body reacted, nipples tightening, thighs aching with the burn of desire. He certainly knew how to take her mind off the small space.

"Glad I could help," he murmured, the hard line of his sexy mouth lifting ever-so-slightly as he gently eased her to her sore feet.

"Tell me I didn't say that out loud," she said, stunned that she would speak before thinking. That wasn't how she operated.

His eyes twinkled with mischief. "I'm glad to be of service. Let me seal the opening so we can't be found and I'll get right on it." His expression turned serious, his strong hands rubbing her arms, giving her goose bumps and making her realize how cool the cavern was despite the Texas heat. "Will you be all right for a minute?"

No. Don't leave me down here. Don't seal us in this tiny hole. Suddenly, the cave felt more like a phone booth than a small bedroom. She swallowed hard, fighting the urge to beg to be taken back above. "Yes," she lied, trying to smile and failing. "I'm fine, now. I'm okay."

He didn't look convinced and reluctantly stepped away from her. "I'm fine," she repeated, responding to the doubt lingering in his eyes, hating that he apparently thought she needed coddling. Her voice turned stern. "And stop looking at me like I'm some needy child. What happened to the cold-shouldered jerk who led me here? Bring him back."

He stared at her, his gaze probing, seeing far too much, she was sure. "He'll be back when you're feeling better and can keep up with him."

"I'm fine!" she admonished in a whispered voice, because noise wasn't such a hot idea considering this was a hideout. "I can keep up just fine."

With an agility most didn't possess, Constantine sidestepped Nicole and jumped in the air, grabbing a steel stake with one hand. He hung there a moment, rotating around to face her. He winked. "We'll find out if you really can, soon."

No doubt of his meaning, her body purred in response. He gave her no chance to reply to the bold statement, presenting her with his back as he climbed the wall. Muscles flexed under his wet T-shirt, denim hugging his nice tight ass. She bit her bottom lip. He was so much trouble, but he might just be worth it. And it wasn't as if he was out of line.

Her little comment had given him an open invitation to come seduce her into calmness, which hadn't been her intention. Not really, anyway. Or maybe it was. Her subconscious was working at getting her what she really wanted—Constantine. She'd wanted that man since meeting him in the bar, despite knowing he didn't fit her perfectly painted world of vanilla sex and strict rules— correction, lately it had been *no* sex and strict rules.

Nevertheless, her current way of living had firmly placed her wild past behind her. And she felt her work helped her make amends—or try to, at least—for what she'd done back then, for getting that damn killer off and watching him take another life. She still had nightmares about the victim.

Her mind's stroll down memory lane landed her

smack-dab in reality. In the small cave. In her present state of discomfort. An easier discomfort than the past held, at least. Her hand went to her throat as she watched Constantine disappear through the same opening she'd just climbed through, leaving her alone. In a hole. A small one. Okay. Maybe this wasn't better than revisiting the past.

Nicole drew a long breath simply because she wanted to make sure there was plenty of air. Then, with supreme effort, she forced herself to stop staring at the exit.

Scrutinizing her surroundings, it appeared she was in a well-planned hideout, not just some cave Constantine knew as a kid. All the basics were present: a small mattress, a small fridge, battery-operated fans and even a few books. Her attention went to each wall as she circled around, feeling as if those walls might close in on her. Her head started spinning, and she knew she was about to hyperventilate. Not something she wanted to do with Constantine nearby. Time to put her relaxation techniques to use.

She quickly sat down on the hard ground, before she fell down, her legs stretched before her. She was too wet, and didn't want to risk damaging the mattress. Resting her head against the wall behind her, her gaze went to the ceiling. Could it collapse? Fall on top of her like the apartment floor had done so many years before? No. This *wasn't* the way to calm down.

Nicole squeezed her eyes shut and tried to focus on something soothing. Birds. Flowers. Sunrises. Instead, her brain took her to an image of Constantine's sweet ass in those dark jeans. Then to the way he'd caught her when she'd jumped, and that sensual slide down that

steely body. Her imagination went wild as she fantasized stripping off his wet shirt, exploring those defined
biceps and hard abs she'd felt through his clothes. He'd
be wild, demanding, incredible in bed. She knew this,
felt it in every inch of her being.

Yes, she missed wild, wonderful sex. But if she
opened the door to a dangerous form of sensual pleasure, would she open the door to that person she'd once
been? The one who'd put power and money, even pleasure, above all else? In her tormented moments, when
the past had twisted her in knots, she had blamed her
ex for influencing her behavior, which was a joke. Her
choices were her own. No matter how much she had
tried, she couldn't deny she possessed a dark, wild
persona that she had tried to smash into retreat. So surrounding herself with people like Constantine, who
could free her of her inhibitions—that was a dangerous
proposition. Dangerous. Yes. That was Constantine.
Dangerously tempting. Dangerously hot.

Vague noises indicating Constantine was moving
around at the entrance drew Nicole's attention. Her
lashes lifted the instant he jumped down to the cavern
floor again. He tossed the rope in a corner, leaving no
evidence above of their presence. He stood at full
height. This space really wasn't so tiny, she thought,
comforting herself with the fact.

Constantine brushed his hands together. "All secure."

She wondered about that. "If you grew up on this land,
don't you think that made it easy for them to find you?"

He walked to the fridge and knelt down, pulling open
the door. "The title is buried too well for that." He removed a bottle of water and offered it to her. "My
grandmother registered the land in her maiden name,

and since then it looks as if it's passed through several owners' hands. Now it's registered under an alias. So, no. The land isn't how they found us."

She accepted the water, surprised it was cold. "How did you manage electricity?"

He patted the top of the fridge. "Special order. Industrial battery-powered. Cost a nice penny, but it's worth it."

Nicole had to agree. She unscrewed the bottle and gulped half the contents while Constantine, squatting down near her, did the same with his own water.

Discarding the bottle on the ground, she said, "I better stop. I'll need to go to the bathroom."

He inclined his chin toward a blanket dangling in front of an opening in the left wall. "Camper toilet."

"You really thought of everything," she said, grimacing at the humble facility. "Still. I think I'll try to avoid using it."

Switching back to safety issues, Nicole considered what he'd said about the property, and vocalized what was running through her mind. "If the title wasn't traceable, then someone on the inside gave away your location."

Constantine finished off his water and discarded the container. Still in a squatting position, he faced her. "Has to be."

"What about Agent Flores?"

Something serious flashed across his face, subtle but distinct, wiped away with the speed and discipline of a man who knew how to live behind an emotional mask. But not fast enough to escape Nicole's notice. She made her living reading people.

"It's not Flores," he said dismissively. "It could have been any of the marshals involved in my protection."

His tone was short, clipped, insistent—even a bit

defensive. Her brows dipped, her eyes narrowing on his face. Deep down, did he suspect Flores? Perhaps, he didn't want to admit it, or just didn't want it to be true.

"Does he know where we are now?" she asked, treading on the thin waters of a bad subject, but also concerned for their safety.

"No one knows where we are but us," he assured her, his voice holding a confidence that soothed her concerns a bit—but not much.

She frowned. "I thought he was meeting us?"

"At a nearby location."

She nodded, relieved.

Their eyes locked and sexual tension spiked as if it had been shot into the room with a cannon. Silence fell between them, heavy with the sudden charge. Constantine was studying her with such intensity she felt as if he could see her soul, unveil what secrets her file hadn't already revealed. Wordlessly, he inched closer.

Instantly, Nicole's heart began to race, anticipating his touch, his nearness. He reached for one of her boots as if he meant to take it off. But that set off one of her phobia alarms, dousing the sexual heat of seconds before. How did he expect her to get out of this place without her boots? Nicole jerked her feet toward her, pulling her knees to her chest and hugging them. "What are you doing?"

"Getting you some comfort. You know your feet are killing you."

"I can't run in bare feet." Running in boots with the heels cut off was bad enough.

"You won't be running anytime soon," he informed her. "We have six hours until we leave. You might as well get some rest and dry off."

Her throat went dry. "Six hours? Several hours is now six? In this cave? Is there oxygen?"

"Yes. Plenty of ventilation points throughout the caverns."

She shook her head. All her efforts at relaxing flew to the wayside. "Still. No. I can't. I...I can't be in this hole that long." Constantine's expression softened. "Don't look at me like that. I am fine. I just can't stay here that long."

He reached out and cupped her cheek with his hand. "You can." Somehow he was closer now. His knees touched hers, a small gesture in a small space. "I'll help you."

"I don't need your help. Just give me some room to process all of this." Crowding her would only make things worse.

But he didn't back off. His fingers slid around one of her calves and inched her pant leg upward; his callused fingers brushed below her knee. Tiny darts of anticipation shot straight to her core. And considering her current state of anxiety, that shouldn't be possible, but yet, he was proving it was. Maybe she didn't need space. Maybe she needed him. She focused on the sizzling sensations he was creating in her, focused on his face so she wouldn't look at the enclosure of the walls. His gaze swept her mouth. "I'm not sure I'm capable of giving you room right now," he said. "I want you too badly, Nicole."

She swallowed at the directness of his words, finding herself mesmerized, lost in those chocolate-colored eyes of his. Desire pooled in her limbs, driving away the fear once again.

Slowly Constantine began to inch the zipper on her boot downward, his fingers trailing her bare skin in its wake. Nicole suppressed a shiver, not willing to let him see how easily he affected her. The man even made removing a boot sexy.

"I didn't want to leave you that first night," he murmured.

The unexpected comment drew a hint of anger from her. Instinctively, she reached forward and covered his hand with hers, stilling his action. In the process, their lips drew close. After hours in the woods, he shouldn't smell good but he did. Spicy and male.

"But you did leave, didn't you?" she questioned, thinking of how he'd snuck under her guard and then left her sitting at that table, feeling a fool. It stung and the memory stiffened her spine.

"If I had stayed, I would have taken you up to a hotel room and made love to you in as many ways as you would have let me." His fingers slid around her other calf, and she couldn't find the will to stop him. "But then, morning would have come, and you would have hated me."

"I should hate you," she whispered, torn between her desire to embrace her attraction to this man and her fear of what doing so might mean. The fear that he might wake a part of her that needed to stay dormant. "What you did was wrong."

His gaze lifted from her mouth. "Do you?" he asked, staring at her. "Do you hate me, Nicole?"

She raised her chin slightly. If he thought lust and admiration, or even like, were the same, he was wrong. Her ex had taught her well—sex could be just sex. "I haven't decided yet."

His mouth quirked ever so slightly. "Good. Then I still have a chance to affect the decision."

Leaning into her, Constantine brushed his lips over hers in a seductive caress that left her wanting more. "Anger can be a powerful aphrodisiac," he murmured softly. "Perhaps you can think of some ways to even the score."

And so the challenge was issued. Play or fold?

Should she hover in this cave and let her phobia get the best of her or show Agent Constantine Vega just how out of his league sexually he really was?

She gave him a sly, sensual smile a second before she nipped his bottom lip with her teeth. "Let's get started, shall we?"

She quickly slid out of his reach and rested against the wall. "Stand up and take off your clothes."

7

"STAND UP AND take off your clothes." Nicole repeated her words, letting them linger in the air, a challenge issued. She knew Constantine wasn't a man who easily gave away control, the exact reason why convincing him to do so now held so much excitement. "If you dare," she added, her words meant to provoke a reaction.

But Constantine wasn't one to be lured into an emotional response. He appeared frozen, no discernible expression on his handsome face. Ah, but she could sense the calculation in him, the struggle within his soul.

Finally he spoke, his voice low, taut. "Once we're even, we're even. The game starts all over again."

"This isn't a negotiation," she said with defiance.

Constantine merely crossed his arms in front of his big, brawny chest and cocked an eyebrow. Without words, he was demanding she concede.

Stubborn man. She had to find a way to steal some of the power. "Fine," she replied. "But I say when we're even."

And yet his expression said he wasn't biting. She made a frustrated sound. "What do you suggest then?"

The corners of his full mouth hinted at a smile, the look on his face now crystal clear. It was hungry, aroused, downright full of sexual heat.

His voice vibrated with that heat as he responded. "We'll both know when we're even." Confidence was clear in more than his words, it showed in his actions as he reached behind him and tugged his shirt over his head, tossing it aside.

Oh, mama, did Nicole get an eyeful of perfection. Constantine's light brown, sun-kissed coloring somehow emphasized the rippling, absolutely drool-worthy abs he possessed. Six-pack be damned. The man had an eight-pack. And nice pecs, too, with just the right amount of hair sprinkled around dark, flat nipples.

But the most arousing feature Constantine possessed thus far was the perfect line of hair seductively trailing downward and breaking at the depth of his inverted navel. It then continued lower until it disappeared into his jeans, a road map to sin and sensation she couldn't wait to explore.

Heat pooled between her legs, arousal radiating through every nerve ending in her body. She was wet and not from the rain. Wet from wanting. A want that had started a week ago when she'd met Constantine, but which had never been fully realized, or fulfilled.

Her gaze slowly slid back up that delicious path of hair. "Finish," she ordered, her voice far more affected than she would have liked it to have been.

"Whatever you want," he said, reaching for the top of his jeans.

"Remember that," she commented, thinking the list of wants was likely to be a long one at this rate. She wanted and wanted. Then, wanted some more. On top. On the bottom. Sitting. Standing. But not yet. Not until she'd tortured him as he had her. Not until that scoreboard was nice and even.

The zipper of his jeans slid down as she impatiently waited for all to be revealed. Unfortunately, he took a short detour, bending down and taking off his boots and socks. That had to be done, she reluctantly admitted, feeling impatient for her prize—a good look at Constantine in the raw.

When finally the denim slid away from his long limbs, so did the boxers. They came off in a swish of movement, leaving nothing but sinfully naked skin and amazing male perfection. Constantine stood before her, his cock jutting forward and all six foot plus inches of taut, mouthwatering muscle—the kind that came from dedicated hours in a gym.

Biting her bottom lip, Nicole debated. Crawl right on over and give him a lick or stand up and do a nice, visual walk around, check out that tight, now naked, ass of his. He deserved to wait for her mouth. Too bad that meant she had to wait, too.

She stood up and quickly made her way behind him. He started to turn. Nicole grabbed his hips. "Don't even think about it. This is my show right now."

"We'd both enjoy this more if you were naked, too."

"I'm enjoying myself just fine," she murmured, one palm gliding over the contour of one firm butt cheek. Damn, it was nice. Tight. Muscular. Her brain went wild with more images: him on top, a mirror overhead, an exquisite view of his body as he pumped into her. Her sex clenched, her body needy for satisfaction. She settled for more exploration, palming the other cheek of that fine ass and then sliding her hands over the back of his upper thighs.

"You *are* enjoying yourself, Constantine," she purred, scooting closer to him, her fingers skimming his waist, teasing low on his stomach, taunting him with how near her hands were to his erection. "Aren't you?" Her teeth scraped his shoulder.

"You're killing me and you know it," he responded, his voice raspy with need.

"Am I?" Nicole questioned in mock innocence, moving her hands from his stomach and walking around to face him. Her eyes locked with his as she refused to look at his cock. "What can I do to make you feel better?"

"Take your clothes off." It was a command.

"No." She smiled seductively. "I'm sure I can soothe your needs some other way, though."

Taking a step forward, she brought his hard length to her immediate left, careful not to touch it with any part of her body. She slid one hand through that dark sprinkle of hair on his chest.

He reached for her and she smacked him away. "No. Don't make me tie you up. I'm sure you have the tools here in your well-stocked hideout."

She scraped his nipple with her fingernail. Constantine sucked in a soft breath, staring at her through heavy-lidded, passion-filled eyes as he vowed revenge. "I'm going to make you pay for this later."

Something told her she'd enjoy paying the price for her behavior, but she kept that as her secret. "That wouldn't be very gentlemanly of you, considering you brought this on yourself."

"I never claimed to be a gentleman, now did I?"

Her lips pursed. "True enough," she agreed, her fingers exploring the muscular contours of his chest before caressing their way to his stomach and brushing the dark hair of his pelvis area. "But then, I'm not exactly the girl next door, either."

"More ice princess," he accused.

Her brows dipped at the accusation, her hand moving swiftly, issuing punishment as it tightly wrapped around his cock. "Does this feel like ice?" she demanded, exploring his length and teasing the head, spreading the drop of dampness there around the smooth tip.

A low sound of pleasure slid from his parted lips, but he still managed a rebuttal. "You're coldhearted, darlin', and we both know it. Otherwise you'd let me touch you."

She pushed to her toes, her fingers still working his cock, her lips lingering a breath from his. "Making you pay for your bad behavior doesn't make me cold. Giving me the control simply makes *you* feel *vulnerable,* and you don't like it."

"I don't feel vulnerable at all," he replied quickly, a glib edge to his voice. "Perhaps it's you who does. Perhaps that's why you're afraid to let me touch you."

Nicole jerked back to glare at him, his words striking an unexpectedly raw nerve that she didn't like one bit. He quirked a brow as if he knew he were right, his expression a silent taunt. Her desire to wipe that sexy, smart-ass look off his too-handsome face sent her to her knees. She'd show him control.

She settled back on her heels, her fingers wrapping around the base of Constantine's erection. Bringing the soft tip of his cock near her mouth so that her breath teased, her chin tipped upward, her eyes found his. "Who has the control?"

His lips were thin, his body tense with anticipation. "You do, *cariña,*" he said gently, his voice hoarse. "I never said otherwise."

Not directly, but he'd inferred his own control. She

lapped at his erection and then denied him further satisfaction. "Yes." The first word held a bite; the rest were an explanation for her actions. "You did."

"If you didn't have control," he spoke through clenched teeth, "I would have my hands in your hair right now, pushing your mouth back to my cock. But be warned." He paused, obviously to let the meaning of his words sink in. "If you tease me too much, I might take *more* than control."

His words both infuriated and scintillated. He was impossible, this man. Most men would beg at this point. He ordered, demanded, threatened to take her. And despite his attitude and his resistance to her command, he made her hot. She could feel her thighs trembling, her sex aching. Damn, the man. He would not win. He *would* beg before this was over.

Nicole ran her tongue down his length, licking him with long, teasing caresses, watching him watch her, aroused by the hunger in his gaze. She worked him with her tongue, stroking over and over, doing everything *but* taking him fully into her mouth. Still, Constantine used restraint; he didn't touch her, didn't ask for what she knew he wanted…what she wanted—for her to take all of him.

Eventually, she gave in to her own desire and drew him into her mouth, pleased when she heard his intake of breath. And while she wanted to see the desire in his features, she found herself absorbed in tasting him. Her lashes settled on her cheeks as she began to suckle him deeply, intent on the pleasure of giving pleasure. Her nipples ached, her clit throbbed. She wanted him to touch her. Still, he did not. His ability to refrain irritated her.

Fully determined to push him over the edge, she took

him deeper into her mouth, her tongue stroking the underside of his shaft. Nicole's hand pumped even as her mouth slid back and forth. His hips began to work against her hand. She palmed his ass, using it to anchor her body as he thrust harder, faster. She could taste the salty proof of how near release he was. So close. Satisfaction filled her, driving her to push him further into his pleasure zone. She slid her fingers along the crevice of his ass, exploring all she could, everywhere she could.

Success came to Nicole when Constantine's hands slid into her hair, as if he feared she would stop working him, stop tasting him. She didn't push his hands away as she might have minutes before. She wanted him to come. Wanted to know she'd taken this powerful male over the edge. She suckled him completely. He was hers now, lost to passion, lost to what she'd taken from him—control. Oh, how she loved it. She'd won the minute he'd touched her head, the minute he'd begun to cling to release.

But just when she thought she'd won, Constantine surprised her, totally taking her off guard. In a movement both fast and hard, he pulled himself free of her. Before she knew it, he'd bent down and picked her up as if she weighed nothing. She either had to let her legs dangle or wrap them around his body, which is what she did. His hands tangled in her half-dry hair, his lips claiming hers, his tongue blasting her with wild fire, stealing her objections with its bittersweet perfection. Everything in her world seemed to melt into that moment, into Constantine's kiss, his body.

Long moments later, he tore his lips from hers. "We're even now. You've thoroughly tormented me."

"I'd only gotten started," she hissed, her voice filled with passion. She wanted to kiss him again.

"I am going to make you come so many times you won't remember your name. Just mine."

His mouth claimed hers in a dominating, hot kiss that left Nicole no room to resist—not that she wanted to. This man's kisses had the unique ability to arouse her entire body. Pure unadulterated lust licked at her limbs, his promises playing in her mind and delivering an extra thrill. Constantine had claimed control, which belonged to her, and she should care. She would care. Right after this kiss.

He seemed to read her mind, tearing his lips from hers. "Nicole," he whispered, his jaw sliding along hers, lips by her ear. "Since we're even now. No more hiding behind that control of yours. It's mine now. *You're* mine now."

8

CONSTANTINE WANTED Nicole's surrender, and he planned to have it this night. He swallowed her objections with another hot kiss, savoring the sweet taste of her. His fingers sprawled on her back, caressing their way over her side, and upward, until he cupped her breast. His thumb slid over her nipple, back and forth, and she rewarded his actions with a soft moan. A moan that spurred his hunger for another one. Yet, he had one thing to attend to first. One absolute must.

Reluctantly, he set Nicole down, driven by the incentive to strip her naked. The barriers had to go, both in the form of her clothing and her games. He'd studied her file. He knew she'd hit the sex clubs with her ex, but he also knew she'd left all that behind years ago. Had covered herself in a prim-and-proper façade—the untouchable ice princess. The idea of making her melt thickened his shaft, arousing him with the sweetness of her submission.

He reached for the buttons of her blouse, impatience making him forgo the effort. "Take it off before I rip it off." He leveled her in a steady look. "And don't think I won't do it. You successfully achieved your goal." Constantine stroked his shaft. "I'm on edge. I want you in a bad way."

She took a step back from him and knelt down, removing her boots, her gaze going to his hand as he stroked himself, her teeth sinking into her bottom lip. "I could have taken care of that for you."

"You will," he said with certainty. "My way."

She stood up, boots and socks discarded, her toes painted a light, delicate pink. Everything about her body was feminine and perfect, soft in all the right spots. But then there was that hard exterior she hid her emotions behind. That had to go. He wanted her in full submission, which meant the walls had to come down.

"What if I don't want to do it your way?"

He quirked a brow at that. "You have something against pleasure? Because, that's what I intend for both of us."

Surprise flickered in her eyes, his response obviously taking her a bit off guard. She hesitated, and then brought her fingers to the silk buttons of her blouse, working them with speed and agility. Her actions, whether she knew it or not, offered her first bit of submission. She'd agreed to allow him his way. They were already making progress.

Without preamble, Nicole finished her task. She slid the blouse off her shoulders, leaving her in a damp, sheer, pink bra that clung to her breasts, the red pert nipples beneath the material exposed for his hungry eyes. Thankfully, she didn't stop there. In less than a minute, her slacks were gone, giving him a delicious view of her long legs and creamy white skin. Next came the panties, the tangle of blond curls drawing his gaze to the V of her body, and he wondered if she was wet—no, he knew she was. He wondered how she would taste, how she would feel wrapped around his cock.

That thought skidded to a temporary halt as that

sheer bra flew to the ground, allowing him to worship those full, high breasts with a more thorough examination.

"I'm all yours, Agent Vega." Her hands went in the air, to her sides, a come-and-get-me invitation. "What are you going to do with me?"

A smile touched his lips with that challenge. Somehow, she'd given in to his demands but still managed to make her own. Damn, this woman got to him.

"On the mattress," he ordered.

Her eyes didn't leave his face. One second, two—she seemed to consider this path of submission that she was treading down. Then, as if she'd decided it, she said, "All right," and settled on the mattress. She sat with her hands behind her, breasts thrust forward, legs slightly parted in a tease of a pose.

Constantine wasn't in the mood to be teased. Not anymore. He found the edge of the mattress with his knees. Before she knew his intentions, she was on her stomach.

His hands braced on either side of her head, his face buried in her neck, cock brushing that lush backside. "My way," he murmured, his nostrils flaring with the sweet scent of her arousal. "You'll like my way, just wait and see."

Slowly, he eased back to his knees, one hand on her lower back in case she decided to turn, the other giving her backside a tiny little slap. Not hard. Just enough to let her know who was in charge.

She pushed up on her hands. "Hey—" The objection became a soft moan as his one palm slid under her stomach, lifting and holding her hips even as he slid a finger across the slick wet heat between her legs, parting her swollen lips. He stroked her sensitive skin, preparing her a moment before sliding his finger inside her.

Her arms went limp, fingers curling in the blanket covering the mattress. A soft moan came purring from that full mouth that had been on his cock only minutes before. He moved the hand he held on her stomach, sliding it to her clit, tweaking and flicking, the action encouraging her hips to arch upward.

Her ass tilted up, giving him better access, inviting him to explore more. He palmed her cheeks, taking a moment to admire that stellar ass in the air before he rotated to lie on his back. He scooted beneath her hips until he found his target. He lapped at her clit and then suckled it. She bucked against him, moving with his actions.

While some women might have stayed on their stomachs, Nicole wasn't one of them. Nor had he expected her to be. She pushed to her hands and knees, but not to escape. She wanted more, spreading her legs, and rocked with the thrust of his tongue. Constantine licked and teased. Her clit was swollen, the delicious honey of her body proof of her nearing orgasm. But just when he thought she'd surely go over the edge, she moved.

Suddenly, Nicole was straddling him. A second later, she took him inside her, surprising and pleasing him all in one action. In unison, they moaned with the impact of her taking his shaft deep inside her body, warm, wet heat consuming him.

She braced her hands on his chest, her voice raspy. "We're trying to get to 'even,' right? You didn't come without me. I didn't want to come without you."

She had wrapped her actions in a sexual taunt, but there was more to it than that. The give-and-take, the status of "even" rather than of one defeating the other—

something about that touched him on an emotional level and shifted the mood.

As if she sensed that and it scared her, she quickly whispered, "That doesn't mean I don't hate you," as her hips worked his cock in a slow, circular tease of a motion. He watched her, enjoying the way her breasts bounced ever-so-slightly with the gentle movement, a visual pleasure, like the rest of her lush body.

"You don't hate me," he said, her actions proving just the opposite.

"I might," she whispered again, but her eyes locked with his, full of intimacy that reached deeper than their connected bodies.

"Don't," he told her firmly. "Don't hate me."

His words altered the mood further, and with the suddenness of a lightning strike in a summer storm, all their power plays, all their games, simply evaporated. Their bodies stilled. There was only this—only the two of them. Perhaps, the uneasiness of their futures, of the way this race for their lives would end, contributed to their feelings. Their connection deepened beyond the physical.

They moved as one. She leaned down as he reached for her. Their lips met in a kiss that was tender, passionate, their tongues stroking, caressing, tasting. Their bodies began a slow dance that matched the rhythm of their tongues. He murmured her name. She murmured his. Their hands explored. He felt her every breath, tasted her every moan. And reveled in the gasp that came a second before her orgasm.

She tensed, burying her face in his neck, her sex spasming around his cock, wet heat begging him to pump harder, deeper. He gave her what she wanted, what he, too, wanted. One hand on her back, he pressed her tight against his body even as he lifted his hips. Suddenly, he exploded, pleasure inching through his groin with an intensity that shook him from head to toe.

Later, they lay there, sated for the time being. She was soft and delicate in his arms. He still wanted her, he realized, arousal forming yet again—his desire to take her was nowhere near depleted. His idea that having her would satisfy his need for her hadn't worked. But even more concerning was what he felt. There was more in the air than good sex. The air crackled with an emotional awareness that he suspected had taken her by surprise as much as it had him. He wasn't a man that did relationships. His career simply didn't allow it. So why wasn't he moving? Why did he want to hold her, to make love to her again?

Before he could give his reaction to Nicole any real consideration, she lifted her head and stared at him, blond hair now dry, wild and sexy around her face and creamy white shoulders. Seconds passed, her attention fixed on his face, probing, intense. Then, without a word, she slid off him and onto her back, arm draped over her face as if she didn't want to be seen. Or perhaps she didn't want to see the ceiling of the cave. Her claustrophobia was still very real; he'd simply distracted her thoughts, her mind, her fears.

It pleased him he could do that for her, that she'd wanted him enough to forget a phobia that clearly controlled her on many levels. An odd desire to pull her close again overwhelmed him. Which was exactly why he didn't reach for her. His life allowed them nowhere to go but to bed. Period. The end.

The dampness on his stomach needed attending, which gave him a "holy shit" reality check. They hadn't used birth control. He always used a condom. Always. Even had one in his wallet, which he'd intended to use. Nicole had overwhelmed him, straddling him like she did, and he'd forgotten himself. Scrubbing his jaw, he resolved himself to the conversation that had to take place.

He reached inside a box that sat beside the mattress, grabbed a small towel and wiped his stomach before moving to Nicole's side. He settled the towel between her legs and held it there, silently asking for her attention.

Her arm lifted from her face, her expression holding a question. "We didn't use a condom," he stated.

She didn't so much as blink. "I take a Depo shot for birth control every three months. Have for years. We're safe. Of course, being responsible adults, we should have used protection for other reasons. Still…" Worry flashed in her eyes. "If Alvarez has his way, we won't see another day, anyway."

The relief he'd felt when she said she used birth control faded with the rest of her words. Constantine recognized the subtle confession she'd offered of being scared over their situation. He was a hard man, not often one to offer comfort, but Nicole touched a softer spot in him, an effect that he wasn't sure he liked. That hardness in his soul had kept him alive a good many times. But somehow it didn't matter where she was concerned, and he didn't know why.

Pulling Nicole into his arms, her back to his chest, a little sound of surprise slid from her lips—surprise that mimicked what he felt inside by his own actions. She didn't resist being held, and that pleased him on a level he preferred not to analyze.

Soon, they were spooning, and inevitably, her soft

curves had his body responding to her nearness. He was hard again and he didn't try to hide it. Instead, he tucked himself between her legs and simply held her. She relaxed against him, again showing him a sign of that trust he'd wanted so badly. Her hard shell had melted away for him. Maybe it would be back tomorrow, probably would, in fact. Probably should. But right now, he wanted to deserve what she'd offered. Resolve formed. Constantine had seen Alvarez destroy too many lives. Nicole wasn't going to be one of them. He'd brought this situation on her; he wouldn't leave her high and dry. And he wasn't about to allow the past three years to mean nothing.

He tucked his chin by her shoulder, her hair tickling his cheek. "Everything will work out. I promise."

9

NICOLE SNUGGLED into the warmth around her, a feeling she clung to, a shelter in a storm. "Nicole. Wake up."

A caress touched her hair, her shoulder. "We have to go soon." The voice came near her ear. Male. Sexy… It jerked her awake. Nicole sat up, looked around her, sucking in a breath that felt a bit out of reach. "Cave," she gasped. "We're in a cave."

"Easy, *cariña*." Constantine was sitting beside her now, pulling her back into those warm, safe arms, against that hard chest she'd explored not so long ago. His hands stroked her hair, her arm. She melted into him as the confinement of the small space worked a number on her nerves. She wasn't weak. She overcame her fear earlier. She could do it now.

Inhaling again, she tried to pull some air into her lungs; she reached for calmness. "I hate this so much."

"I know. We're leaving in about an hour from now."

"I didn't mean this place, but the way I respond to it. I hate it." Why had she just admitted that? Nicole gently pushed out of his arms. "I'm okay." She scooted to the edge of the bed, telling herself the exposed feeling was her nudity when she knew it was her emotions. Something was happening with Constantine. She'd gone to him in lovemaking, and now she'd opened up about her inner fears.

He slid a sheet over her shoulders, as if offering her shelter. His hands stayed on her shoulders. "We all have things we wish we could change about ourselves."

She shifted her position to face him. "Yeah?" She didn't wait for an answer. "What would you change?"

"Being too weak to kill Alvarez when I had the chance." Constantine scooted to the edge of the mattress.

"That wasn't weakness," she assured him. "Doing what is right is harder than doing what you desire." She knew this firsthand. Knew it because she'd lived a life where money and excitement, even sex, drove her actions. Where winning wasn't about what was right. It was about what it could do for her.

He didn't comment, and for some reason, she thought he regretted his admission as much as she had hers. She opened her mouth to ask why and shut it again—the sight of Constantine pushing to his feet, his jeans in his hand, stealing her words. He was naked and, with the flex of all that muscle, breathtakingly male.

As if he wanted to tempt her into an outright erotic fantasy, he gave her a show, pulling on his underwear and pants, his long legs, and tight ass, too spectacular to ignore. Amazingly, she managed to reach for her bra and slip it on, thankful it was almost dry. Somehow, she even pulled on her wrinkled mess of a blouse.

Her gaze swept the broad expanse of his chest, the bulge of his arms. She had slept like a baby in those arms, despite the cave. How long had it been since she'd slept in a man's arms? Two years? Three? *It doesn't mean anything.* Nor did the desire she had for this man. He wasn't pulling her back into her old life, her old world. She was stronger now. She could separate her sexual needs and wants from her other choices. In fact, wasn't Constantine helping her to see that?

Constantine grabbed his shirt and pulled it on, covering up the chest and arms she'd been inspecting. Nicole finished dressing, easing her pants over her hips. She had justified her actions by her need for a distraction. Who would have known a hot man could put an end to her claustrophobia, or at least put it in check?

Nicole was about to put her boots on when Constantine kneeled beside her and stilled her actions with his hand on her leg. He indicated a box beside the mattress. "There are bandages and ointment in there. It will help ease the pain."

His touch sent a barely concealed shiver down her spine. "Thanks," she said, cutting her gaze away from his too-attentive eyes.

While Nicole bandaged her foot, Constantine filled a backpack with supplies and then sat down next to her.

"Hungry?" he asked, offering her a granola bar.

Her stomach rumbled loudly and they both laughed. A smile touched his lips. He was handsome when he smiled, and the awkwardness of their confessions faded away.

"I guess that answers your question," Nicole responded, pressing her hand to her abdomen and accepting the food.

He grabbed a couple of bottles of water from the fridge and they ate in silence. Nicole could barely wait to leave. She thought back to how understanding Constantine had been of her phobia. Her ex rarely crossed her mind these days, but he did now. He'd been impatient over her claustrophobia, irritated because their sexual escapades never included her being tied up, and embarrassed when she panicked on business flights. She hated those memories, but considering their current life-and-death circumstances, Constantine's patience had been a surprise. He was a contradiction, demanding and hard, yet gentle and understanding. It made her curious about him.

"You must have spent a lot of time out here to know the land so well," she commented, hoping for a look inside his past.

"I moved in with my grandmother when I was twelve. My grandfather died in Vietnam and she never remarried." He cut her a sideways look. "My mother died of breast cancer and my father threw himself into his work after her death. He died a year later on an undercover assignment."

"FBI?"

"Yes."

"You must have been proud of him to follow in his footsteps." She and her father hadn't agreed on a lot of things these past few years, but he'd been her idol growing up. Seemed Constantine had felt the same about his father. She continued, "I went into law because of my father. Of course, I ended up choosing a different direction for my career. I'm sure you read all of that in my file."

"I did," he admitted, not appearing uncomfortable with her private details. "Must be awkward to have your ex still working with him."

Nicole shrugged. "I've learned to accept being the outsider." She fiddled with the paper wrapper around her granola bar. Even her mother acted as if she'd betrayed the family.

"Your sister is going to work with them now, isn't she?"

"My file has a little of everything, doesn't it?" She didn't wait for an answer. "I don't want her to but she won't listen. She wants to be the defense attorney no one can beat and have a paycheck that proves it." She shifted the conversation back to him. "Do you have any siblings?"

"No," he said, his tone clipped, as if she'd asked something offensive. Perhaps a sign he was done with the personal talk.

Either way, all this chatter about the darkness hidden in his past, in her past, took her mind back to something he had said right before falling asleep. "Everything doesn't always work out no matter how hard we try."

A shadow flashed across his face. "This will," he said, his gaze locking with hers, that edge of danger she'd seen in him on other occasions igniting like a sudden flame. "I walked away from too many chances to kill that man for us to fail now. I'm getting you to that trial, and you're going to convict him. I won't let him walk away."

Nicole's eyes went wide. Something about his last words, his promise that Alvarez wouldn't walk away, bit into her nerve endings. What exactly did that mean? Was he saying he'd kill Alvarez if she failed to convict him?

Before she could reply, a beeper on Constantine's watch went off and he pushed to his feet. "Time to go."

She stood, feeling lighter with the prospect of escape from the cave, but no less concerned about his comment. "I'm all for that."

"Stay here," he ordered, as he had so many times in the woods. "I need to check the surface for unwanted visitors." He didn't wait for an answer; he started up the wall. All the warmth of before had fled. He was cold, calculating, a soldier on a mission.

Constantine was willing to do whatever it took to take down Alvarez—even become a murderer himself. She'd walked the line between right and wrong, and it was a dangerous place to balance. A place that would steal your soul if you let it and she almost had. Nicole realized why Constantine scared her so much. He was walking that line just as she had. He was walking it and she was afraid he'd pull her along with him.

AN HOUR AFTER traveling in the pitch-black night, Nicole found herself, once again, hiding in the bushes, Constantine by her side. The rain was gone, but a starless, moonless sky spoke of more to come. Eerie silence thickened in the humid night air, heavy and ominous.

With an incline of his head, Constantine directed her attention to what appeared to be a small trailer park only a hill beyond the cover of the woods.

"We're meeting Agent Flores there?" she whispered.

He pointed, indicating lights bobbing and weaving down the old dirt road leading to the trailers. She swallowed hard, her stomach fluttering with worry. He thought something was wrong. She could tell by the stiffness of his body, and by the uneasy vibe he gave off since departing the cave.

He didn't look at her when he spoke. "Stay low and let's move." And then he was gone. Nicole scrambled forward as he disappeared beneath the waist-deep grass, making fast tracks down the hill. She bent down, following his lead. The possibility of another snake crossed her mind, but she shoved the worry aside. She had to keep up with Constantine. He was moving so fast that she had to push to catch up. And then, as if slamming into a wall, he stopped. Chest heaving, Nicole skidded to a halt and kneeled beside him.

She watched in silence as a nearby car's lights went off, and the passenger's door opened, inviting them inside. A safe haven was only a few feet away.

Nicole grabbed Constantine's arm, silently asking for confirmation that this was their ride. He gave her a quick nod. Before she could fully embrace the glory of being saved, he took her hand and pulled her forward, making a beeline toward the car. And that was when all hell broke loose.

Out of the silence, the sound of motorcycle engines blasted the air, and Nicole knew without being told, they were in trouble, about to be found. Their ride was so close. Nicole clung to the hope of shelter, but to her horror, Constantine tugged her in the opposite direction, detouring from the nearby safety that merely taunted her.

Moments later, Constantine maneuvered her behind a trailer, completely out of Agent Flores's view. "Why aren't we with Flores?" she whispered urgently, watching as Constantine bent down and yanked a piece of underpinning from the trailer.

"They didn't find us on their own." He motioned her forward, into the darkness beneath the trailer. "Go."

She would have argued but gunfire filled the air, followed by the sound of a motorcycle engine growing closer. Without further hesitation, she scrambled beneath the house, Constantine at her heels. Cobwebs skimmed her face and she bit back a yelp. Constantine quickly put the siding in place not a second too soon, as a motorcycle sped directly by their location. Any fear of what was in the darkness disappeared as Nicole realized how close they'd come to being discovered.

Her heart pounded furiously in her chest, her mind racing just as wildly. Sooner or later they would be found. What would happen to them? What about the innocent people in this trailer park? Did Constantine think Flores had led the attackers to them on purpose? Surely not. That had to be his gun firing at the bikers. Someone in the trailer park might have called the police, but they were so far off the beaten path. Would it be soon enough to save them?

A penlight came on, barely illuminating Constantine's face. He motioned her forward. "This way," Constantine whispered, leading her to the front end of the trailer, weaving through the darkness as if it were daylight.

The sound of a motorcycle neared again…no, two— two motorcycles. Constantine waited until they passed and then eased a small patch of siding away to scan the situation beyond it. Nicole scooted forward and did the same. Unbelievably, they were right beside a pickup truck.

"Bingo," he murmured, glancing at her. "The minute you see the passenger's door open, start running and don't stop until you are inside."

As usual, he didn't wait for a reply. He was already on the move, slipping through the opening that seemed too small for him. She tried to get her mind around everything that was happening, trying to make it some nightmare, not her life. But it was her life.

She watched Constantine stealing the truck. Pressing her fist against her chest, she thought her heart might explode. She let out a sigh of relief as the car door opened. She sucked in another breath before wiggling through the hole, not giving herself time to think about what might happen if this went bad.

Nicole cleared the trailer and crawled toward the truck. A motorcycle sounded again, then another gunshot. Her heart lurched. Digging her knees into the ground, she pushed forward. Finally, she was there, climbing into the truck. She pulled the door shut, ducking below the window, and not a moment too soon. A motorcycle sped by, but this time it stopped. Male voices sounded, pieces of the sentences reaching her ears. They were going to start a search on foot.

Constantine worked the wires beneath the dash, his head low. "Good," he said of the conversation they'd overheard. "We want them on foot so we get ahead of them." He motioned with his chin. "There's a gun inside the bag on the seat. Get it out. You're going to need it."

She did as he said, removing the hefty handgun that was sure to fire with a kick that would jolt her from here to Mexico.

The truck's engine roared to life. Yes! Nicole screamed in her mind.

Constantine floored the accelerator, the tires on the truck screeching against dirt and rock as he made a rapid turn to the left.

A motorcycle appeared by her window; the driver pointed a gun at her. Her hand tightened on her gun.

Constantine swerved at the rider and the bike crashed. One danger gone. More to come.

Nicole slid open the rear window of the cab; a pair of bikers were on their tail. Aiming, she shot at the tires of the nearest motorcycle. She hit her target, but the backfire of the weapon sent a jolt of pain up her arm, through her shoulder and into her chest. Worth the pain though. The biker skidded across the terrain and crashed as the other one had.

She steeled herself to fire again, but was thankful when the second pursuer dropped back before she had to. Sinking into her seat, she let out a breath. "I think they're gone."

"They'll be back."

She glanced over at him. "I figured, but let me revel in momentary success."

"Those were Carlos Menchaca's men," he announced. "I'm sure you've seen his name in the file."

"Menchaca," she said, ready to focus. "Right. He runs drugs along the border for Alvarez."

They'd cleared the woods now; a highway was within sight. "Carlos will see what I did as a personal betrayal. He considered me a friend. I fooled him when no one has. He'll come after me for that reason alone. Pleasing Alvarez will be nothing but bonus points."

"I thought he was part of the Alvarez takedown?"

"He was supposed to be. Somehow he slipped away the night of the bust. I'd hoped he'd be found before he became a problem. But since that little fantasy hasn't come true, I have only one option."

Nicole swallowed. She knew what he meant. He was talking about going after Carlos.

Life as she knew it seemed to get more complicated every second she was with Constantine. Every time she turned around, he was walking that thin line she tried to avoid, stepping in the gray instead of living with black and white, right and wrong.

It was easy to decipher Constantine's reasoning without even hearing him speak. The world would be a better place without men like Alvarez and Carlos, and she didn't disagree. But she also knew the law existed for a reason. To protect people's rights. When you let it fade away, the system, and its foundation for existing, did as well. Which left her with the question of how to handle Constantine. She glanced at his ruggedly handsome profile, not sure of her answer.

Should she support him? Try to convert him to the straight and narrow? But then, a man like Constantine could make a woman forget herself. Maybe she should run like hell before she was the one to get converted.

10

CONSTANTINE CLUTCHED the steering wheel of the Mustang Coupe he'd nabbed about twenty minutes outside of the trailer park. Had Flores—one of the few people he trusted—betrayed him? He didn't want to believe that. Flores had been like a brother, a close friend, one of the few he'd ever called a friend in fact. But then, his world was corrupt; his life, riddled with enemies.

"No answer," Nicole said, dialing one of the disposable cell phones they'd bought at a twenty-four-hour, touristy-type store. They had both gotten T-shirts and cleaned up. Nicole had even bought a pair of tennis shoes. "Not from my boss or my sister. I can understand my boss. He's probably at the hospital with his wife, but I'll feel better when I hear he's keeping me on this case. I'm more prepared than anyone to put Alvarez away. Even with a slight delay of the trial from all of this I can be back in Austin and started in a week. If it goes well, we can keep the jury already selected."

"I'm sure your boss will see that," Constantine said, his reply weak, distracted. Nicole's concern for her family proved how different their lives were. Back at the cave he'd almost convinced himself they were alike, that maybe he was ready for the kind of connection they shared. He was already leaving the agency, after all. But that wasn't the case. His enemies would always be in the shadows, a threat to him and anyone near him. Hell. Carlos would kill Nicole just to prove Constantine couldn't protect her. If he knew Constantine had feelings for her, that would only give him more satisfaction.

"I hope so," she said of her boss's understanding, drawing him back into the conversation he'd all but forgotten. "I mean, what's the point in putting another D.A. in danger. I'm already a part of this, and I've accepted being in hiding until the trial."

Nicole had asked him a million questions about where they would hide, and how they would pull off getting back for the trial. She tried to control things when she felt uneasy, he'd figured that out, both in and out of bed. It didn't bother him. In fact, he rather liked knowing he'd broken the barrier in bed. But why the idea of doing so outside of it appealed to him, he didn't know. Not that it mattered anymore. He had no business getting close to her. At this point, he had to stop the bond that was only beginning to take form between them before it was too late. He was a one-night stand and nothing more. She needed to know that. Hate him if she had to, but do so alive.

He cast her a sideways look; her hand was shaking ever-so-slightly as she punched the cell numbers again. With a jerky movement, she shoved hair behind her ear. "My sister—"

"Is in Hawaii celebrating the results of her bar exam," he told her, his voice full of a calm certainty. "She's safe."

A frustrated sound slid from her lips. "I'd feel better if I heard her voice. I told you my father would refuse security. It figures he's the only one I've been able to reach."

Constantine tried to comfort her. "At least he agreed to send your mother away, and he's trying to reach your sister, too. Even though Alvarez is standing trial, his reach is far and deep. And his crew know what's expected of them." He switched gears. "Dial Flores again, will you?"

She thumbed through the list of numbers and did as he asked, handing him the phone. After several rings, Constantine gave up, grinding his teeth to keep from cursing.

"You're worried," she said, and he could feel her looking at him.

He focused on the white lines of the highway rather than her, not sure what she wanted him to say. He was worried and he didn't want to lie to her. Before morning he planned to be a long ways from here. He'd already told her he had a boat at Padre Island that was well-stocked with supplies, and even plenty of cash.

When he didn't answer, she probed. "Can't you call someone else?"

"I could," he agreed reluctantly, "but I'd rather not until I figure out where the leak is. Carlos found us somehow."

"Could they have followed Flores?"

"Maybe." Of course, he'd considered that option, but Flores was careful—too careful for stupid mistakes. Constantine didn't say anything more, didn't want to add to her concerns.

"Try to get some rest," he suggested. "We have a few hours before we stop."

He needed to think. If Flores had betrayed him, where did that leave him? There were higher-ups he could go to, but again, who did he trust?

She let the seat ease backward and turned on her

side, facing him, her hands under her cheek. As she watched him, she asked, "This won't end at the trial, will it?"

His gut twisted with that question. She didn't understand how true her assumption was. He'd learned the hard way. He'd lost a brother when the legal system failed. "Even if we put away Alvarez, Carlos will keep coming. For me. For you. For anyone he can bleed for vengeance. So in answer to your question, no, it won't end with this trial."

She was silent for several seconds. "Capture him and I promise to convict him."

He glanced at her. She couldn't promise that. She knew it as well as he did.

Darkness slid through him. He was angry. At himself for failing his brother. At the system for failing his brother. And at Nicole for working both sides of that system.

"You and I know that attorneys can get criminals off. You've done it yourself." The air chilled with his words but he pressed onward. "I get that you think you're cleaning your soul by doing things by the book. But frankly, sometimes that book does more harm than good."

"So murder is okay if you do it for the right reason?"

Who was she to judge him? "I'm not after a big salary or even recognition. I simply want Alvarez and Carlos stopped."

"You bastard," she hissed at him. "That was a horrible thing to say to me."

"I'm just speaking the truth, sweetheart, and I didn't say you. I meant in general. Tell me. How does the possibility of letting someone like Alvarez or Carlos walk on a damn technicality make you feel? It's okay to let them go and damage more people's lives? You can live with that?"

"No one says they will walk. But what would you have me do? Fabricate evidence to ensure convictions?"

"If you know that person is guilty, and you know they will kill innocent people, how can you let them get away with it?"

Her voice was a bit breathless. "I don't know what happened to you while you were with Alvarez, but whatever it was, it's destroyed your perspective." Her tone grew stronger, more forceful. "You can't work within a system you don't support. You can't convict criminals when you are willing to become one."

"Don't you get it?" he asked, laughing bitterly. "The system asked me to become one. That was the only way to take down Alvarez. You use all the wrongs done by people like me to make your cases and yourself feel safe and honorable. I am what I am because of the system. Hate me if you will, but if you fail to convict Alvarez or even Carlos, I'll finish the job for you."

He focused on the road, knew he was right about what he'd said, yet he could feel the heat of her angry stare, feel her judgment, her disapproval. And it bothered him. He tightened his grip on the steering wheel. Why? Why did this woman get to him so damn badly? Why did he care what she thought?

She said nothing more, turning away from him, offering him her back. He'd succeeded in pushing her away. Good. So why did he feel like absolute shit?

NICOLE JERKED AWAKE, her sleep restless, her conflict with Constantine—along with worry for her family— tormenting her thoughts.

She sat up as they pulled into a hotel parking garage. "Why are we stopping?"

"I need rest and to eat a real meal." He didn't look at her as he pushed the car door open and stepped outside.

She sat there a minute, debating how to handle him, noting his wording—"I" not "we." The tension from their argument remained as thick as the Texas heat, oppressive and ready to suffocate any cordiality left between them. And it bothered her. It bothered her in a big way.

She'd spent considerable time during the drive pretending to sleep, fretting over their argument. Trying to figure out why their conflict mattered so much. He'd been a complete jerk, saying things intentionally to hurt her. Painful things that hit a nerve because they were the same words she said to herself deep in the night when sleep refused to come.

Constantine pushed the limits of every rule he came in contact with. He was wild, living dangerously close to the edge of trouble, justifying his actions in the name of honor. He represented everything she'd been running from in her life. *Running* being the operative word. But it seemed she couldn't run from her past anymore. Inviting a renegade FBI agent into her bed proved that. What that meant exactly she hadn't decided. All she knew was she would not be intimidated or crushed by a few harsh words spoken by Constantine or anyone else.

And no matter what his claim, he'd rather defeat Alvarez and Carlos in a courtroom than outside the law. Otherwise, he would have taken one of the chances he claimed he possessed while undercover to kill them. He did want to do what was right. He was simply feeling the effects of three years in a hellhole.

One thing was for sure, Nicole thought, reaching for the door—they had to make this work. She couldn't run from him now. Nor he from her. They were stuck together for at least a week, maybe more. Constantine had to include her in the decisions being made. She wouldn't be shut out.

She walked to the rear of the vehicle and stopped in front of him. His hands were on his hips, the look on his face impatient. He wanted food and rest; she wanted answers. "Where are we exactly?"

His eyes glinted with steel. "An hour from the boat."

"Then why stop? I thought you wanted—"

"To eat and get some rest."

Her lips thinned, her eyes probing, searching the hard expression in those eyes for some vestige of peace. But she found none. No emotion, no sensuality, no comfort. He'd shut her out. "Constantine—"

He reached in his pocket and handed her a black wallet. She looked at it, confused. "Not Constantine," he said. "Michael Rodriquez."

She opened the black leather cover and stared at her own picture next to the unfamiliar name. "Sarah Rodriquez?"

"Right," he said. "You're my wife." With that said, he motioned toward the elevator. "Let's move."

She lagged several steps behind him, about to reach for his arm and demand they clear the air. But one look around the garage, cars lined up one after another, and she took off after him. Anyone could hide behind, underneath or even inside one of the vehicles.

She caught up with him in a half run. "We have no bags. Don't you think that looks funny? Even our clothes—"

"Looks like we've been rolling around on the beach.

Two lovebirds who can't get enough of each other." He kept walking. "Don't overcomplicate matters."

She made a frustrated sound. "I'm just trying to survive here."

He stopped in front of the elevator and punched the arrow button. "Then do as I say."

He stepped into the elevator, faced forward and pushed the button to hold the door. She didn't move; her blood boiled at the bossy arrogance of his attitude. He had made the act of entering that elevator some sort of submission on her part.

A car sounded behind her. His gaze went beyond her shoulder and then back to her face. His voice was low, but as intense as if he had shouted. "Get into the elevator."

Her heart skipped a beat just thinking about someone approaching. She moved forward. When she turned and could see the garage again, she was relieved to notice only a woman and a small child getting out of a car. She let out a breath, thankful she was safe.

Constantine let go of the elevator button, and stepped backward. "You relax far too easily. Everyone—man, woman and child—is a potential enemy. Don't forget it."

If everyone was a potential enemy, was he? He'd lied to her and done a split-personality routine. She was confused, tired. She didn't know what to believe at this point.

The elevator doors opened to display a busy, though very average-looking lobby. People seemed to be everywhere. Nicole stared into the hustle and bustle with concern. "Shouldn't we be secluded somewhere?"

His arm wrapped around her, pulling her close to his

side. The warmth of his touch seared her straight through her clothes. Anger apparently did nothing to lessen his impact on her senses.

"Safety in numbers," he said, leaning down so that his breath tickled her neck, warm and inviting. The sensation brought back memories of intimate moments, of forbidden touches.

She tried to act like everything was fine. Like a woman would act with her husband. That almost drew a laugh from her. Marriage often came with tension. If her marriage had been any indicator, strain between her and Constantine would seem quite the norm.

Nicole clenched her teeth. Being this bitter wasn't what she wanted. And she really thought she had those old feelings beaten. She forced her demons away and smiled at the desk clerk.

Minutes later, she stood next to Constantine as he slid a room key into a door handle. Awareness charged the air and defied the coldness of his demeanor. They both knew they might disagree on the justice system, but there was one area they agreed on completely—sex. Something their one-bed suite was going to make hard to ignore.

11

CONSTANTINE SHOVED open the door to the hotel room, as aware of Nicole's nearness as he was of his next breath. More aware actually. Breathing came without thought. Every second he was near Nicole, he desired her. Hell. He could feel her body next to his even when he wasn't touching her. When he wasn't lusting after her, daydreaming over how he'd take her if he ever got her naked again, guilt nipped at his gut over what a complete, total ass he'd been to her, bringing up her past as he had.

She'd slapped him down for walking outside the circle of acceptable that she'd drawn around herself—making him the bad guy, good enough to fuck and nothing more—and it pissed him off. Actually, he'd welcomed a reason to be angry, darn near desperate to put some distance between himself and Nicole. To stop whatever connection was forming between them before it clouded his judgment and he forgot how dangerous he was to her. People wanted him dead. Alvarez. Carlos. Plenty of others he'd taken down, too. She'd attacked his beliefs and given him the fuel to shove her away—and he'd pounced on it, holding back nothing. Living in Alvarez's world had taught him how to be a coldhearted bastard, if it had taught him nothing else.

He stepped aside, allowing her entrance into the room and motioning her forward. She hesitated, her gaze flickering over his face for a quick moment, as if she, too, knew the implications of the two of them alone, in a hotel room. Her chest lifted with a breath and she entered the room.

His gaze drifted to the sexy sway of her hips and the pert lift to that lush backside. There was no escaping the attraction between them, and his groin tightened with the proof. He wanted her. His body didn't care if they were from different worlds.

This crazy attraction he felt for her wreaked havoc on his mind and body, had him rationalizing her resolve to follow the system as easily as he did for working around it. He was, after all, aware of the pain hidden behind that façade of prim and proper—he'd used it against her in their argument. Only she wasn't prim and proper, and their lovemaking, like her past, proved as much.

Following her into the room, he shoved the door closed and locked it. She'd positioned herself at the window, her back to him. The room shrank—if that were possible—as he eased toward the bed, sexual tension charging the air, damn near combustible in its presence. Staying in a hotel room with Nicole, and keeping his hands to himself, was going to be a real task. No. Worse. His own little piece of hell.

"Don't get too comfortable," he said, not that she appeared to be trying. She felt what he did. The room was small. Too damn small. "We need to go grab some clothes and food."

The curtain she'd been holding fell back into place as she turned to face him, her eyes going to his, avoiding the bed. "Is it safe to go out?"

Her nipples pebbled beneath the cheap T-shirt and his gaze went where hers had not—to a king-size invitation to rip her clothes off and have his way with her. Was it safe to go out? Hell. Was it safe to stay *in?* His cock thickened, pressing painfully against his jeans. No woman drove him to this kind of insanity. He'd be dead a hundred times over if he let his damn dick control his decisions.

He ground his teeth as his gaze inadvertently flickered across those tight little nipples again. His cock throbbed. With a verbal backlash, he took out his growing frustration on her. "I don't plan to question your legal abilities. It's my job to get us out of this alive. We're safe. We'll stay safe. And we will get to the right people to get the trial under way. How about you let me do it without questioning my every move?"

He didn't expect her to cower at his attack, nor did she. For an instant, the gentle curve of her brows dipped, and then her expression transformed to an outright scowl, her petite hands jabbing at her curvy hips. "You didn't question my abilities?" she asked incredulously. "Do my job, you said, or you'll take matters into your own hands." Her tone mocked him. "In other words, you manipulated me into feeling I was responsible for either outcome. If that's not an inference of you questioning my abilities, I don't know what is."

"It wasn't about questioning you," he countered. "It's about reality. Alvarez cannot walk free."

She opened her mouth to speak and then tightened her lips into a thin line. An inhaled breath followed as she appeared to consider her words. "I'm going to detour from a subject we obviously can't agree on and say this. My life is on the line. Don't expect me to blindly follow your lead. I have a right to be informed about my own safety. Would you expect any less if you were in my position?"

They weren't talking about him and he almost said as much. Instead, he forced himself to consider her words. He wanted her to trust him, and, yes, do so blindly, because he was good at his job. But regardless she'd be foolish to operate without caution. Their history together had been a short, intense one, full of adversity.

He softened toward her. What was it about this woman that could take the hardness inside him and tear it down?

"Try," he said, his voice gentle, the edge gone. What else *could* he say? "All I ask is that you try."

Her expression slowly eased. Anger and accusation disappeared as she crossed her arms in front of her chest. She was still on guard, but not on attack. "I will. I promise."

That was something, he guessed. They'd both compromised. Now he needed some space before softness turned into something else…maybe comfort, more likely sex, exactly what he was avoiding. Sex with Nicole was as big a distraction as a man could conceive.

A quick glance at the clock told him it was only eight in the morning. "Let's make this supply run fast. If we step it up, we can make those phone calls, eat and sleep, all by sunset."

"And then?" she asked, and laughed, realizing she was already questioning him again. "Sorry. I can't help myself."

"I know you can't," he said, a smile tempting his lips, but he was too damn tired to see it through. But not too tired to admire Nicole's smile. Disheveled and without makeup, she still glowed. "But I don't have an answer for you. Not yet."

"Not until we know when the trial is." It wasn't a question.

"Exactly," he agreed. "For now, let's take care of ourselves and get some food." *Before I forget myself and feed my hunger with you.*

NICOLE STOOD IN the tiny store watching as Constantine threw chips, candy and all kinds of junk into a small basket. "I thought we needed supplies?"

"This is the critical stuff," he said with complete seriousness in his tone, grabbing a bag of Doritos. He appeared to be a man on a mission—to achieve a heart attack. "We should pick out some clothes."

She blinked at that. "From here?"

"Right," he said, pointing toward several racks of souvenir-type clothing. Holiday garb at best. "Grab some T-shirts and shorts for us both. A couple of pairs. And shoes. No sandals. I'm a size twelve."

She reluctantly headed to the clothing racks, wishing for something more substantial, but thankful for anything at this point. A bath and clean clothes of any type sounded like heaven.

Beside the racks, several tables held shirts and shorts. Nicole began inspecting the contents, selecting a few items. Two extra-large shirts for Constantine, two mediums for her, two pairs of print shorts for her. She picked dark blue parachute shorts for Constantine. His options were limited. It was either the dark blue kind or orange floral ones, which she couldn't imagine him wearing.

But then he deserved the bright neon flowers for taking those personal jabs at her. Smiling, she put the blue shorts back and grabbed two pairs of the orange.

She was reaching for a pair of tennis shoes, when a voice beside her asked, "Souvenir shopping?"

Nicole looked up to find herself staring into the interested eyes of a gorgeous, beach-blond god of a guy, not more than twenty-two. He towered over her at a good six foot plus and offered a charming smile. He was dressed in shorts and a tank top that showed off his picture-perfect body. Most women would be drooling—but not Nicole. She'd found a rather consuming interest in a certain tall, dark renegade, sporting a bad attitude and a hot temper.

Still, a friendly face was welcome about now. Nicole returned his smile and answered his question. "Something like that."

"Yeah, me, too." He reached for a T-shirt. "Gotta take gifts back to the family." He studied her for a long, thoughtful, flirtatious minute…which was insane considering she looked like absolute hell. "I'm Rick."

"Nice to meet you, Rick." His comment about family had her thinking of her sister. She so needed to hear her voice.

"My mom is the hardest," he commented. "I never know what to take her."

She thought of her own mother—another bad subject. Nicole barely knew her anymore. Leaving the family business had ruffled a lot of feathers. Nicole hadn't even done family Christmas the year before, using work as an excuse. Her attention returned to Rick. "What's so hard about buying for your mother?"

"For one thing," he commented, hand waving over the table, "she doesn't wear T-shirts."

"No T-shirts?" Nicole teased, mustering a half smile. "Well, that only leaves you one option."

His brow lifted. "Which is?"

"A coffee cup, of course. Everyone knows they get a T-shirt or coffee mug from a vacationer."

They laughed together. "You won't convince my sister of that. She thinks shoes are the perfect gift, no matter what the occasion. If it can't be worn on the feet, it isn't worth having."

"Smart girl," Nicole said, offering her approval. "A personal favorite of mine as well."

"Of course." His expression said that was a given, a moment before he changed the subject. "How long you here for?"

The question took a second to register, her mind still on her sister. "Um," she said, trying to think how to answer, "I haven't decided."

A disbelieving laugh filled the air. "You're at the beach and don't know how long you're staying? That's kind of unique. Most people come with a plan."

A hand touched Nicole from behind, sliding to the small of her back, branding her with possessive heat. Constantine stepped to her side, but she didn't glance at him. Shock, and a hint of panic, rolled across Rick's face. A look that only deepened as Constantine said, "She does have a plan." His voice was hard, deep, sexy. "Being with me."

Rick gulped. "Oh," he said. "I'm sorry, man. I wasn't… I mean…"

Nicole opened her mouth to say something, anything, that might save the poor kid some embarrassment. But Constantine put his arm around her shoulder and pulled her under the nook of his chin. That contact stole more than her breath; it stole her attention from saving Rick. Constantine's long legs pressed close to hers, electricity shooting through every inch of her body. It was a simple gesture commonly shared by couples but there was nothing simple about her reaction.

"Sorry if I interrupted," Rick said, his voice nervous as he started to back away, dropping the shirt to the table. Clearly he was ready for a fast departure.

Why did Constantine find it necessary to intimidate such an innocent young kid? It made no sense. She didn't take him as the kind of guy to throw around his strength in such a way. Anger began to build inside her.

"We should be going," Constantine said, his tone hinting at demand.

"Me, too," Rick agreed quickly, and he was gone, rocketing through the store as if he'd been set on fire.

Nicole whirled on Constantine and would have stepped out of his reach but he grabbed her waist, holding her so close their legs were entwined, hips aligned. The heated words she'd been ready to spurt a few seconds earlier took extra effort to crawl past her lips.

"What's your problem?" she whispered.

His tone was low, lethal. The look in his eyes full of impatience. "You don't seem to get the message. *Anyone* and everyone is a potential threat."

"He was a kid," she argued. "One you just about scared the hell out of."

"You've been in the system long enough to know what criminals are capable of. Alvarez isn't above anything. He'll do whatever it takes. Even pay an innocent kid to ID you."

"That kid was not with Alvarez."

A woman with dark hair and glasses walked past

them. Constantine's eyes followed her, suspicious, his expression cautiously assessing. Did he know something she didn't? Tension slid through her body as the taste of fear thickened in her mouth.

Nicole watched Constantine watch the woman. And then watched his gaze slip back to her. Their eyes locked. Desperately, she searched his face, looking for a hint of what might come next. And what she found turned her fear to boiling hot anger.

He was messing with her head, trying to prove a point. "Don't do that." She glared at him. "I despise stupid head games."

Leaning a bit closer, he said, "I assure you, this is not a game. Alvarez leaves a trail of bodies wherever he goes." Seconds passed, the mood shifting in some indescribable way, still tense, still charged. And then, unexpectedly, Constantine's attitude softened, much like it had in the hotel room. "I don't want you to be one of them."

She gave him a dubious look, her throat suddenly parched. Was that tenderness in his eyes? Worry? Surely not. And why did the idea of such things warm her inside? They'd had sex. The smoldering tension between them said they wanted to have sex again. It meant nothing. Or did it? When she delved into the depths of Constantine's eyes, she felt something more than attraction, a vague sense of kindred spirits that betrayed their exterior differences. Something that scared her as much as Alvarez did, simply in a different way.

Pressing past her emotional questions, Nicole had to admit Constantine delivered a persuasive argument. She couldn't be selective about her caution. She had to start thinking with the kind of ultraconservative mind-set she used in the courtroom.

"You're right," she admitted. "I'll be more careful."

A look of surprise flashed across his face before he gave her a quick nod. "Good. Let's finish shopping and get out of here." He turned away from her then, but not before Nicole noted the confusion in his eyes.

At least she wasn't alone in her emotional turmoil. It appeared Constantine didn't know any more what to think about her than she did about him. They were trapped together for the time being, running from Alvarez. They could escape from Alvarez, she had confidence in that. But escaping whatever was happening between the two of them…she wasn't sure they could.

12

ON THEIR WAY back to the car, Nicole felt Constantine's hand on her arm, gentle, protective. She appreciated it more than the heat he fired within her. Nicole appreciated his presence, his strength, his willingness to risk his life to save her. They were in this together, and she needed to act that way.

Once they were settled, Constantine locked the doors. Silence filled the air, unspoken words between them thick with the need to be voiced. Nicole took the lead. "I guess I don't want this to be real. Intermittent denial."

"You don't seem to have that issue where your sister is concerned." It wasn't a question.

Looking after her sister had always been a priority. Their parents had pushed them both so hard. He had no idea how much truth rested in those words, or maybe he did. The man survived undercover by reading people.

She laughed, nervous about how easily he saw through her, saw things no one else did. "I know. It's crazy. I blame it on the need for food and sleep."

Quickly he turned the engine over. "I can fix that."

She wasn't ready to end this conversation. Not yet. Her hand went back to his arm, drawing his gaze to hers. He went still, utterly still, his scrutiny so intense she found that the attention stole her breath.

Somehow, she forced herself to speak. "Thank you for what you've done to help me. For what you're doing to protect me and my family."

Silence followed, thick, potent. Finally, he said, "You know how you can thank me?"

Why did this seem like a trick question? "By convicting Alvarez?"

"Like this." He moved then, pulling her close, those strong arms embracing her, that firm, perfect mouth slanting over hers. That possessive, sensual tongue sliding against hers. One hand slid to the side of her face, his fingers entwined wildly in her hair. Nicole decided that agreeing with Constantine, as she just had, came with perks. He might be bad for her in theory, but he was oh-so-good in many other ways. And right now, with all that was going on, all that they faced, she wasn't sure she had it in her to deny herself this man. She wanted to kiss him, touch him, *trust* him. The future be damned—for all she knew, she wouldn't even have one.

Seconds passed as they kissed, sultry seconds where his mouth seduced her into surrender. And, damn, surrender felt uniquely sweet, a pleasure no other had ever given her. When he tore his mouth from hers, he leveled her in a sizzling stare.

"There are a hundred reasons why we shouldn't be doing this," he said.

In a barely audible voice, she agreed, "At least that many."

"You're a control freak."

"So are you."

"We can't both run the show."

That made her smile, her mind going to the cave, to their power struggle. "It was fun trying the first time."

A hint of a smile touched his lips. "Which brings me to my point." His mouth brushed hers, as if he couldn't resist one more taste, one more touch. "We'd be better off leaving what happened in that cave, in that cave."

"Right." She squeezed her legs shut, those memories sending an ache straight to her core. "Better off."

Neither of them pulled away despite their declarations that they should resist one another. Their lips lingered a breath from touching, electricity darting around them, through them.

"But the truth is," he admitted, "I've got too many other fires to put out to fight this one. I want you, Nicole. How do you feel about that?"

Wet. She felt wet. And ready. Like they were on the same path of satisfaction, both in mind and body. "I feel…ready to go back to the hotel."

Approval glinted in his eyes, and he scooped in for one last brush of her lips before reluctantly releasing her. He shifted gears and turned on the radio.

"Hurricane Ed appears to be headed straight for the Gulf of Mexico and speculation puts Texas in the line of fire."

Constantine cursed under his breath and Nicole knew why. It appeared passion wasn't the only stormy weather they had to ride out. Even Mother Nature seemed to be aiding Alvarez, stealing their safe zone. Because now there was no way they could hide on Constantine's boat, their ultimate destination, in the middle of a hurricane.

Nicole couldn't help but wonder how big this storm was going to be before it was over.

BACK AT THE HOTEL, Constantine curbed his more primal instincts, at least for a short time. He had business to get done, critical issues, like a shower so he wouldn't stink to high heaven. Most importantly, there were phone calls and plans to be made—when to return to Austin, how to do it safely. The best steps to take to ensure Alvarez was convicted not freed. Not that any of that made him forget that long, hot kiss in the car. How could he? Nicole was on the bed next to him, and despite the room-service cart in front of them, a bed was a bed, suggestive as ever. And her shorts allowed him to admire those long, sexy legs more readily.

He glanced down at his tropical shorts and grimaced. She'd gotten quite the laugh when he'd appeared wearing them, so much so, he'd had the feeling something was up. When he'd said as much, she'd admitted buying them to spite him. Her amusement had been, well, amusing. He didn't get amused. But then there was nothing normal about what he felt for Nicole.

He had to have her again.

Nicole had somehow managed to eat her strawberry waffle in between calls to her father, her sister and now her boss. Constantine finished off a biscuit loaded with butter and honey right about the time she ended the conversation.

"That sounded encouraging," he commented before licking a drop of honey off his thumb, erotic images of licking honey off Nicole's body sending his pulse racing.

She tossed the cell phone on the bed, oblivious to how hot she made him without any effort, which somehow only made him hotter. "It was," she agreed. "Dean not only said I should remain on the case, he promised to fight to make it happen. He's calling the judge personally with a promise that he will take over if I can't make the trial—which is, of course, almost unheard-of. It will speak volumes to the court about how important Dean feels I am to this case. But it also means a delay of two weeks because of his wife's cancer treatments."

Constantine brushed crumbs from his hands, pleased with the announcement. "And my testimony?" he asked.

"He was sold before I brought it up. A guy named Nelson called Dean this morning. Told him if you were alive, you were needed."

Constantine paused, a glass of orange juice halfway to his mouth. He set the glass back down. "Why would Nelson be calling instead of Flores? If this Nelson is who I think he is, he has been working a drug task force in the Houston area, only helping with aiding the Alvarez takedown. No direct involvement."

Nicole continued to recount her conversation. "Dean mentioned something about how that came about. Flores took a bullet in his shoulder and spent the night in the hospital. That's why you couldn't reach him. So Nelson transferred into the Austin office and assumed his duties."

The food in his stomach downright rolled. "Wait one damn minute. Filling in for Flores or replacing him?"

She hesitated. "Dean used the word *replace*. I admit that seems a bit odd."

"You can say that again." Constantine rubbed the back of his neck, a weight exploding onto his shoulders. He'd met Nelson once when he'd been arrested along with a bunch of the Alvarez gang. He'd known Constantine's identity and he'd maintained the necessary secrecy throughout the process. But he couldn't trust him. Not when someone on the inside was dirty.

Nicole pushed the breakfast cart out of the way to

face him, one knee on the bed, one foot on the ground. "I know you trust Flores, but is this an indication someone else doesn't? That they think he's the leak?"

He wanted to say no, but that would be a lie. "Either that or they want a fall guy in case things turn sour. You know how the story plays. This is high profile with lots of press. Someone has to go down if the operation fails."

She didn't immediately respond, the scrutinizing look she leveled his way a little too probing for his comfort. He scooted back against the headboard and kicked his legs onto the mattress. He let his head drift backward, lowering his lashes, withdrawing into a shell so he could deal with what he'd learned. His mind raced wildly with the implications of her news.

Suddenly, Nicole was there, refusing to be dismissed. She straddled him, sitting across his lap. His head shot up as her hands settled on his chest. Despite his state of mind, instantly he was hard, the thin shorts they each wore offering no barrier between their bodies. He could almost feel the damp heat of her body. Was she wearing panties?

Nicole hugged herself, covering her breasts and successfully drawing his attention to her face. "Are we okay?" she demanded. "Should we leave? What did she say?"

Hands by his sides, he resisted touching her, resisted reaching for her on all levels. Life had taught him to remain guarded. Caring meant pain. Loss. But she'd offered him insight into her life that a file folder couldn't give him and he wanted to know more. And right now, he didn't care that he'd have to share his own feelings to get to hers.

"Who betrayed you?"

"Does it matter?" she asked.

Yes. "It matters."

Shadows floated in her eyes, seconds passing, and he began to think she wasn't going to answer. Then she said, "My ex. It was my ex. Only not in the way you might think. It wasn't about other women. I let him pull me into his world and convince me it was mine. In the end, it was his, and what I wanted didn't matter. I was a tool to get to my father. Ironically, he never needed me for that. He's still my father's protégé." Pain flashed in her expression before she refocused on him, her hand brushing his jaw. "So you see. I hope Flores didn't betray you. It's clear you don't offer trust easily."

He didn't deny the truth. Nor did he point out their similarities in that way. Instead, he found himself taking her hand, bringing her knuckles to his lips and then peering up at her from where his lips prepared for another taste. "Did you love him?" He didn't know what in the hell made him ask the question, nor did he know why her answer felt so important. But it did.

A hint of tension betrayed her body. He kissed her knuckles again, then her wrist. Slowly, her muscles softened, her expression softer now, too. "I guess it depends on how you define love. I said the words. I thought I meant them. Now…now I don't know. The only love I know for sure is for my family, my sister especially. We're very close. My parents don't approve of my life so it's strained." The tone of her voice said she regretted that last admission and she quickly fired a question at him. "Have you ever been married? In love?"

Constantine searched her face, saw the loneliness in her eyes. He knew then, that part of their connection was that solitude they both had lived. He pressed her palm to his, thinking how petite and somehow fragile she was, yet how brave in actions and spirit.

And when he would have dodged this question from another, he found himself answering honestly. "No, to both." Guilt twisted in his gut over the lie he'd told in the cave. Lying to her in that bar had been survival. Lying in that cave had been cowardly, his way of hiding from what he didn't want to face. He tried to shove it aside, and focused on telling her what she wanted to know. "I'm thirty-five and have spent my entire adult life in the FBI. My job doesn't exactly make me Prince Charming." He hesitated, recognizing some internal need to clear the air. "I lied to you." She gave him a startled look and he blasted forward, continuing before he could talk himself out of it. "I have a brother." He had spoken in the present tense before he could stop himself. But talking about Antonio as if he were gone bothered him.

"What? You said—"

"I know what I said. It's an automatic answer I give. It's easier than saying he's dead."

She sucked in a breath, understanding filtering into her expression. "How?" She whispered the question.

"He arrested a guy named Martini, not as heavy an operator as Alvarez, but still a big fish. Based mostly in San Antonio."

He hesitated and she commented, "I remember hearing about that case."

He continued, eager to get this off his chest. "Martini was released on a technicality and…" His voice trailed off. "You can guess the rest."

Her eyes went wide. "Oh, God." Her voice shook. "He killed your brother."

Constantine's gut twisted in knots. Years had

passed and this still tore him apart. He couldn't speak, so he nodded.

She leaned forward, hands gently cupping his cheeks, the tenderness in the act squeezing his heart. It had been forever since he'd told anyone about his brother, years since he had felt a touch like this one, so caring, so understanding.

"That's why you threatened to kill Alvarez and Carlos," she said, her gaze searching his, pouring into his, reaching into his soul.

Somehow he found his voice, and confessed the sin that devoured his sanity every day of his life. "I was in deep with Alvarez when my brother died. I couldn't go to the funeral." To his horror his voice cracked. "I should have been there." He squeezed his eyes shut. "He was my kid brother. I should have saved him."

"Oh, Constantine." She brushed her lips across his. "Don't do that to yourself. I know it's torture, but you can't carry that blame all your life. It'll tear you apart."

He was surprised to see tears in her lovely blue eyes. "Easier said than done. We both know *you* blame yourself for getting a man off who killed again. I've seen how you turned your life around because of that case."

"That's different." Her lashes fluttered, her eyes lowering to his chest, gaze averted. "You had nothing to do with your brother's death. I got a high off being the best at my job, at being the most successful defense attorney in Texas." Her lashes lifted, tears tumbling over her cheeks. "I was self-centered and greedy, and someone died because of it."

She swiped at her tears. "I'm sorry," she said. "I'm tired and emotional."

Regret filled Constantine. He should never have

brought this up. He didn't blame Nicole for being a defense attorney, nor did he blame her for being good at it. The system was the system and he was frustrated with it. Perhaps, had he met her before, he would have felt differently about her. But they were the same in what they ultimately wanted—justice for the victims of Alvarez, and those like him. Nicole's regret over the past was eating her insides out and he knew this. Just as his past had left a hole in his gut. "I'm sorry," he said. "I didn't realize how raw this was for you."

She inhaled a shaky breath. "Don't apologize. It's hard to get past the blame, Constantine, but you won't do it by pretending it doesn't exist. I know from experience that if you don't deal with what you feel, it gets worse."

Noting the stronger tone of her voice, he recognized her effort to pull her emotional armor into place. He didn't want it in place. They had a lot in common, the two of them. They were both alone, both torn up inside. Right now, he wanted only one thing. To get lost in her. To forget everything but this woman.

His hands went up her back, molding her close, easing her mouth to his. "I'm going to make love to you, now, Nicole." His mouth slanted over hers in what he meant to be a gentle kiss…but they were both wound tight, both in need of a release, a place to put the pain and loneliness. Outside a storm threatened their hiding place. Inside, passion thundered, threatening to take him to a place he'd never traveled before. A place he didn't dare name. A place he didn't dare go. A place he burned to make his own.

13

CONSTANTINE KISSED Nicole with a fiery passion borne of pent-up emotions. Why they'd surfaced now, why with this woman, he didn't know, nor did he care. Because he felt her giving herself to him, felt he was her escape as much as she was his.

For every stroke of his tongue, every touch of his hand, she gifted him with some unique response: a sigh, a caress of her tongue, a nip of her teeth. Yes, he was hers for sure.

He barely remembered removing his shirt, though he remembered every caress of her hands on his bare skin. She sat back, facing him, her lush backside framing his cock, teasing him with delicate pressure. Silky blond hair fell around her face in sexy, wild array. She wore no makeup, her ivory skin flawless.

Eyes the color of a perfect sky stared at him, eyes brimming with a message—with freely offered passion, with tenderness he'd never accepted from another, yet he wanted it from her. There would be no games, no battle for control this time.

Her fingers latched on to the hem of her shirt, and she tugged it over her head, tossing it to the floor. She wore no bra, her high, full breasts displayed for his viewing. Her nipples swelled and tightened under his inspection. But when he would have reached for her, he held back, willing himself to refrain from making demands, to enjoy every moment of her, every way possible. For now, he was savoring the view she made, which was tightening his groin.

A soft sound escaped her lips as she took his hands, pressing them to her breasts. Her mouth lingered near his. "I *need* you to touch me," she whispered, her teeth scraping his bottom lip, arching into his palms as he kneaded.

The boldness of her actions shot fire through his veins, but it was her words, and the passionate way she stared at him, that ran over him like a firestorm. Need. She needed him. Who was he to deny her?

He pressed her breasts together, using his thumbs to tease the erect rosy-red peaks of her plump breasts. She rewarded him with a moan, the response rocketing to his cock, thickening it with demand.

Burning to hear another, to pleasure her, his head lowered, his tongue lapping at one pert nipple and then suckling. Her hands went to his head, fingers sliding into his hair. She covered her other breast with her hand, aiding his efforts. He pulled it away, his mouth finding the unattended nipple, lavishing it with attention.

She whispered his name, and he lifted his mouth to hers, somehow knowing a kiss to be her demand. Her lips were sweet, her tongue caressing his with careful strokes. He traced the gentle curve of her jaw with his fingers, before traveling the sensual line of her neck.

For a moment, he stared into her heavy-lidded eyes, touched by what he felt for this woman. As hot as he was, as much as he wanted inside her, the tenderness between them consumed him—it was unexplainably perfect. Their passion was both erotic and innocent, simple and complex. The emptiness inside him cried out, twisted in his gut, reaching for her.

Constantine kissed Nicole again, desire pulsing in his blood, warning that a kiss would soon not be enough. Nevertheless, he found himself lingering, savoring these moments. The taste of her, the feel of her skin against his, her breasts pressed to his chest.

Slowly, Nicole lifted her lips from his, depriving him of her kiss. She searched his face, emotion brimming from beneath her dark lashes, emotion that made words unnecessary. She was looking for confirmation that they felt the same way; he could see it in her eyes. There was something about her in that instant, a vulnerability that spoke to him with such completeness that he thought he might be looking in a mirror, seeing himself. A likeness that drove past the sexual desire they shared—a likeness that wrapped around them and made them one. He wanted to be one with her, buried to the hilt, the warmth of her surrounding him.

As if she read his mind, she inched away from him, reaching for her shorts. He did the same, working to shove the material down his hips. But his eyes remained riveted on Nicole. She wasn't shy about her body, as sunlight spilled through the window, and she showed no hesitation at being exposed. By the time he'd discarded his clothing, she was crawling toward him, her breasts swaying seductively with the action.

She bit her bottom lip as her gaze swept his erection. Her tongue darted over her lips, and he groaned, the action reminding him how sweet it would be on his cock. She settled at his right hip, again on her knees. Her left hand brushed his shaft and his heart jackhammered, his eyes shutting for a second before opening. He watched her hand travel over his length, the view of the exploration stimulating him as much as the touch did.

Delicate fingers swept up and down his shaft, trailing the ridge around his engorged head and then spreading the dampness gathering there, the proof he wanted inside her. But he held himself in check, aware that the wait would only make the bliss all the more powerful.

There were a million erotic things he wanted to do with this woman, but right now, right *now,* he simply wanted to be a part of her. He wanted to be lost inside the wet, perfect heat of her body.

"I *need* to be inside you." The words were guttural, hungry, and he hesitated no more. He pulled her across his lap, holding her weight as her hand wrapped around his shaft, guiding it to her core.

She acted swiftly, as if she, too, felt the urgency, slipping the head of his shaft inside her, and then starting the seductive slide downward. Adrenaline sizzled through his nervous system, stealing his breath. By the time they were one, pelvis against pelvis, a whisper from kissing, he was on fire—blazing red-hot and emotionally charged. In a far corner of his mind, he recognized this was sex—where the hell had the emotion come in to play?

His nervous system was in overdrive. Every breath he managed came with a sensation, a charge. And from the heavy rise and fall of her chest, she felt the same. But for some reason, he wanted to know for certain.

Intentionally, he kept his body still, fighting the urge to pull her hard against his cock and thrust into her. Instead, he brushed the mass of shiny blond locks from her creamy shoulders and caressed his way down her arms. She shivered and leaned into him, her arms wrapping around his neck, nipples brushing his chest. "What are you doing to me?"

And so he had his answer. She was as lost in him as he was in her, equally uncertain about why or how. He'd bedded his share of women. Hard and fast, slow and easy. Though never, ever, had he lost himself by merely having a woman take him inside her. But he was lost now.

His fingers brushed her nipples and then tugged lightly. A gasp escaped her lips, and the muscles of her body tightened around his cock. He tugged a bit harder and she moaned, her muscles squeezing harder this time. Suddenly, her mouth was on his, her tongue delving past his lips, her hips beginning to rock against him.

Pleasure shot through his groin and exploded throughout his limbs, threatening to consume him. But he wanted her pleasure more than he wanted his own. He continued to tease her nipples, applying pressure, twisting and tugging. She gasped against his mouth.

Constantine started to pull back, afraid he'd hurt her, but her hands closed over his, her tongue stroking him with a hungry kiss. There was no pain in the kiss, only pleasure. She rocked forcefully now, and he pumped his hips to match her movements. When he had the position perfect, he used his mouth to suckle one nipple, then the other.

Her gaze fixed on his mouth as his lips worked against her breasts, her heavy-lidded gaze saying she was aroused by watching. The harder he suckled, the faster she jerked her hips, adding to the pressure on her nipple. He caressed and tweaked the other nipple, pleasuring her again and again, but also needing more.

He continued to suckle her nipple, but his hands went to her hips, wanting leverage. He thrust upward, and pulled her down at the same time. She cried out and grabbed his arms, using them to push herself down on him. Thrust, push, thrust, push. The room filled with noisy heavy breathing. They were wild with passion, fulfilling their need. To be closer, to move faster and harder. Nicole screamed pleasure, softly pleading for him not to stay.

Tongues tangled as they devoured each other, hands everywhere, bodies bucking, primal animals in heat. Abruptly, he felt Nicole stiffen, heard her gasp a second before her nails dug into his shoulders. Spasms closed down on his cock, pulling at him, taking him. She shook with the force of her release. He took control then, grinding her hips down against his, pumped once, twice, three times—and then he exploded. The power of his release ripped through him from deep in his groin, and he, too, was shaking.

When eventually they stilled, their heads buried in each other's shoulders, surreal silence surrounded them. They inched apart enough to stare at one another, searching each other's faces. What had happened between them? That was the unspoken question in the air. Whatever it was had Constantine's insides quivering in an indescribable way.

Nicole reached up and softly traced his brow, tenderness sweeping across her face, and then she rested her head back on his shoulder. His heart squeezed; his chest was tight. He could barely breathe. This connection, this bond, had to be a façade, the result of the adrenaline rush of being on the run. Didn't it? But deep down, he knew it was more. He couldn't fall for Nicole. He was nothing but trouble. Hell. He didn't want to be worried about someone. He didn't want someone else to fear for. That part of his life was behind him.

"What are you doing to me, woman?" he whispered, repeating the question she had asked of him earlier.

Nicole didn't respond, but she tightened her arms around him. Seconds passed and they relaxed into each other, their breathing the only sound in the room. Holding her in those moments came with a sense of peace and serenity, an experience unique, never to be reproduced. There might be other special times, other amazing moments. Or perhaps there would be none. That possibility clenched his gut. He didn't move, nor did she. Perhaps they were both afraid of ending something that might never be repeated.

Constantine contemplated sleeping with her in his arms, recognizing his desire to keep her close. He had even started to ease them both to the mattress when a sudden pounding on the door brought him back to reality. He tensed, preparing to defend Nicole. Her fingers pressed into his shoulders, and she leaned back to search his face, anxiety shining in the depths of her eyes.

"Housekeeping," someone called through the door, the female voice carrying a heavy Hispanic accent.

Nicole expelled a breath, her body going limp with relief. Constantine felt nothing of the sort. They'd only checked in a few hours before. Housekeeping should know this. Besides, pretending to be "housekeeping" would be an easy trick to get the door open. With regret, he motioned for Nicole to climb off him; her expression quickly filled with worry again as she scrambled for her clothes.

Constantine snatched his shorts from the floor about

the time the knocking started again. "Housekeeping!" A key was being jiggled in the lock. Thankfully, he'd flipped the inner latch so it would catch before the door fully opened.

"Ahora no," Constantine shouted out, telling the woman in Spanish "not now," dropping his shorts in exchange for the Glock on the nightstand.

He bolted across the room, arriving at the door as it came open, hitting the barrier of the steel latch. Constantine peered through the opening, the housekeeper looking at him through the crack. He repeated his prior words and went on to demand why she was even present when they'd only checked in hours ago.

The woman responded to his demands with an on-slaught of Spanish, which concluded with an apology. Constantine relaxed marginally and sent the woman away. He slammed the door shut and slid the lock into place. Then he turned to stare at Nicole. Still on the mattress, she was on her knees, her shirt in place but nothing else, nipples peeking beneath the thin material, and clearly showing the dark triangle between her legs. His gaze devoured the sight, his body stirring.

Nicole hugged herself. "Are we okay?" she demanded. "Should we leave? What did she say?"

"We're fine," he answered, starting toward the bed. "I was being safe. Better safe than sorry."

"You're sure?" she asked, as he set the gun back on the table. Her eyes scanned his body, widening ever-so-slightly as she noticed the growing girth of his erection.

His knees hit the mattress. "As sure as I can be under the circumstances."

"On a scale of one to ten—"

Constantine cut her off with a disbelieving laugh

and reached for her. She frowned, her hands pressing on his chest a bit defensively. "What's so funny?"

"You trying to find control someplace that it can't be found." He tugged at her shirt and pulled it over her head, finding no resistance on her part. His palms framed her breasts and then slid to her cheeks. "I said, we're fine."

She didn't look convinced, and he shook his head at her stubbornness. Grabbing the blankets, he motioned for her to join him underneath. They crawled under, lying down, heads on their pillows, facing each other.

"I know it's hard to be calm, but try."

She nibbled her bottom lip a minute, and he could see by her expression that her mind was racing. Another worry-laden question followed. "Shouldn't we flip on the news and find out about the hurricane?"

Remarkable, he thought, and found himself wanting to smile again. "Later." The mattress was starting to call him to slumber. "Come here." He urged her to turn around, her back to his chest.

She snuggled against him without argument, a surprised sound sliding from her mouth as he settled his erection against her backside. "You're hard again." She said the statement as if she'd just noticed, which they both knew wasn't the case.

"Hmm," he murmured. "I seem to have an unlimited appetite for you, even when I'm exhausted. In fact, I was thinking of some delicious ways of using the rest of the honey that room service brought with my biscuits."

"Were you now?" she purred seductively.

"Oh, yeah," he whispered near her ear, as he nuzzled her neck. "It'll taste much better on you. I'm sure of it."

A soft, sensual laugh slid from her lips, and she

snuggled against him, her hips doing a sexy little wiggle. Then she sighed and seemed to melt, as if she were giving herself to the bed, to the need to sleep. Maybe to him. Yes. To him. Another time he would analyze why that idea appealed to him so much.

A full minute passed in which he assumed she was falling asleep until her tentative voice filled the air. "What was his name?"

His gut clenched. He hated talking about his brother. "Antonio."

"Younger or older?"

"Younger by five years. He was twenty-seven when he died two years ago."

One second, two. "You felt protective like I do about my sister."

"Yes," he whispered. "Kind of ironic considering he was tough as nails and made his living protecting others."

She maneuvered to her back and touched his cheek before settling on her side to face him. "The horrendous crimes we see give us a reality no one else has. We know how easily life can be stripped away, without reason. How can we not? I eat breakfast, lunch and dinner reading case files telling gruesome stories with graphic pictures. You see those things firsthand. I can't imagine what that is like."

"It's part of our job," he said, realizing he'd had this conversation once before. With his brother.

"The job doesn't come without consequences. We have to deal with what we see, and it's not always easy."

But it was easy for him. He felt nothing. Hadn't since about a month after his brother's death. It was how he'd survived Alvarez. "Somewhere along the line I found a way to switch it off. I feel…nothing. Not really. Not often."

She made a disbelieving sound. "Yes, you do. I've seen the intensity in your eyes when you talk about Alvarez and Carlos. You found a way to tuck your emotions into some corner of your mind, but the feelings are still there."

"Is that how you deal with your past?"

"Yes," she replied, a hint of pain lacing her tone. "I'll be glad when I get as good at it as you, though. Being responsible, even indirectly, for a murder makes for a lot of sleepless nights. I keep thinking if I win enough cases, put enough criminals behind bars, I'll forgive myself, but so far it hasn't happened. Maybe it never will."

Guilt stabbed at his gut yet again. "I shouldn't have brought that up in the car. You were right. I acted like a jerk."

A smile touched her lips. "Yes. You did."

"Does it help to know I regret it?"

"Not much, but some." Her fingers slid into his chest hair, her eyes dropping to her hand.

He pulled her close, hand on her firm backside. "You're cutting me no slack, I see."

"It was mean," she said, her gaze lifting.

"I know. I'm sorry."

"Are you? Or do you deep down despise me for what I was?"

Pulling her leg over his, he slid his now throbbing erection back between her legs. "Does that feel like I despise you?"

"Wanting to fuck me is no indicator."

Her words, cold and bitter, caught him off guard. Before he could stop himself, he admitted what was better kept unspoken—since there could be no future for them. "There is more to what is going on with us than simply sex. And we *both* made assumptions about one another that weren't exactly true." His knuckles caressed her cheek, his voice tender. "You're brave, sexy and, I am beginning to learn, way too hard on yourself." He framed her face with his hand and gently met her lips with his. When he pulled back to look into her eyes, he saw that same vulnerability he'd seen while they were making love. If he didn't get her to sleep soon, he was going to find his way back inside her again. "We should rest."

She nodded. "Yes."

He eased onto his back and took her with him, settling her head on his chest. She wrapped her leg around his, and the act warmed him inside out. Yes, this woman did things to him. He ran his hand down her back—this moment in time too perfect to explain. He stilled, savoring the feeling.

Far too soon, they'd have to face the hell of running for their lives again. So, for a short window of time, at least, he wanted to pretend his world wasn't one big hole of darkness. And somehow, Nicole made that possible.

14

ON THE THIRD DAY of basically living in the same hotel room from sunup to sundown, Nicole blinked awake, giving the bedside clock a blurry-eyed glance. Eight in the morning. Only ten more days until they headed back to Austin for the postponed trial. Only. Right.

Weeks of her life would be lost before this ordeal was over. Not that she minded being with Constantine. He'd become quite a delicious distraction.

And speaking of her distraction…beside her, Constantine stirred, pulling her into his arms. They rested, side by side, facing each other, heads on pillows. Feigning sleep, he kept his eyes shut, as if he had reached for her in slumber. But she knew better. She could feel his attentiveness.

Having spent every waking moment with him for these few days had taught her a lot about him. You could learn a lot about a person in those circumstances. Hours of doing nothing but making love and talking. Even watching the entire first season of *24* had unveiled little pieces of his life, telling her more than he probably even realized.

Thunder rumbled outside, reminding her of the hurricane, drawing her back into the present. She started to move, intending to find the remote and turn on the television, but she was stopped by Constantine, who shackled her legs and held her in place.

"Where are you going?" he asked, his voice rough from sleep, but his reflexes alert, telling her she was right about his feigning sleep. He was wide-awake and had been for a while. Of course, he was always on edge, ready for trouble. She took comfort in that. Then again, she hated it for him, and was coming to realize he had less peace in his life than she did, and she didn't have much.

Recognizing this sent a wave of tenderness through her, and Nicole placed a quick kiss on Constantine's forehead. "I'm trying to find the remote. There should be a solid storm path now." He hesitated and then released her legs. Nicole smiled and climbed over him to reach for the remote on the bedside table, the covers falling away from her naked backside. As he caressed her ass with his palm, she laughed and eyed him over her shoulder. "You are such as ass man, I swear."

"I worship all parts equally. I think I've proven that."

"Nope," she said, scratching the remote and then sitting back down. She cast him a teasing sideways look. "You're an ass man and I challenge you to prove otherwise." Scooting up against the headboard, she took the sheet with her and pulled it to her neck. Her teeth chattered as she flipped through the channels. "You turned the heat down again."

"You weren't complaining last night," he pointed out, sitting up on the side of the bed. He was referring to the marathon sex they'd shared mere hours ago.

True enough. She wasn't complaining one bit. Well, except for the honey. It had been great until after the orgasm—okay, two orgasms. Then, it had been sticky.

"Will you turn it up now?" she asked, a little plea in her voice.

He stood up, displaying all his taut muscle and naked glory. Would she ever be tired of seeing that man without clothes? "You didn't have to ask," he commented. "I was headed there now."

Inwardly, she smiled at that. "Thank you."

He winked at her and a thrill raced up her spine. Such a minor thing. It would have zero impact coming from someone else, but it set her on fire coming from Constantine. She couldn't seem to sate the desire. Somehow, it simply burned hotter.

She watched him cross the room, feeling surprised at how caring he could be, despite the darkness he carried inside him. No male in her life had ever given her a secure feeling. That Constantine could do so under such extreme circumstances said something. She wasn't sure what. Maybe she'd been hungry for a human connection, maybe they both had, and the situation had made it possible.

She refocused on the television and flipped through the stations, stopping on the weather and turning up the volume.

"There is no dodging this bullet for the Texas coast, as had been hoped. The good news is the storm has weakened to a category two with winds of one hundred and twenty miles per hour, expected landfall late tomorrow afternoon. Evacuation—"

Nicole muted the sound, more interested in what Constantine had to say at that point. The threat of the storm had left them in limbo or they'd already be at his boat.

"You said anything over a category one would put us on the road again," she reminded him. "So this means we're leaving, right?" He'd told her he wanted to make just one final stop, claiming the more they moved around, the more chance of making a critical mistake that gave away their location.

"Right," he agreed, messing with the thermostat before giving her his full attention. "As soon as we take care of some critical business." Offering nothing more, he headed toward the bathroom.

She gaped at his back. "What does that mean?" But she was talking to air. He'd disappeared around the corner, and a second later, the shower came on.

Nicole shoved aside the blanket and shivered. Hugging herself against the cold, she stomped into the bathroom, finding Constantine already behind the curtain. "What critical business?" she demanded. "There's a hurricane coming. A big one. We have to leave."

The curtain moved and he peeked out at her, water clinging to his long, dark lashes. Then he disappeared without a word. She flung her hands out to the side. Unbelievable! She climbed into the shower and faced him, instantly finding herself pulled into his arms, one of her legs lifted to his hip, his body fitted to hers. He was aroused, and suddenly she was, too.

She gave him a frustrated look, pretending to be unaffected by their naked bodies pressed together. "Why didn't you answer me?"

Mischief danced in his eyes. "Because I knew you'd get in the shower if I didn't."

Secretly, she thrilled at his response. "Answer now."

"First and foremost, we have to make fast tracks down to the boat and pick up the money and supplies, before we can't get to it at all. Then, we do some fishing, prior to disappearing until the trial." His hand slid around her backside, fingers trailing the crease low enough to make her moan.

She reached behind her and covered his hand, struggling for coherent thought. "Stop. I can't think. What the heck are you talking about? Fishing?" Surely, he was joking.

He grinned, apparently pleased with that answer. "Then don't think."

That wasn't an option and he damn well knew as much. "Explain!"

A low, sexy chuckle slid from his lips. "We're going to catch us a bad guy," he said, derailing any further questions by kissing her, a fiery kiss that carried her into oblivion.

For only a moment, he raised his head, giving her a sizzling look before saying, "This is one of those times you have to let me do my job." The words had barely left his mouth, when he penetrated her, sliding his long, hard erection inside her and stealing her breath. Suddenly, the meaning of his words wasn't clear.

Did he mean, trust him to do his job, to get them out of here safely? Or trust him to give her an orgasm? Because as he began thrusting in and out of her, she was quite certain, the orgasm part was a sure thing.

AN HOUR LATER, Nicole sat next to Constantine, in the little Mazda he'd produced from who-knew-where, eating burritos from Taco Bell. The wind whipped furiously around the car; the clouds were dark and ominous, but no rain fell. According to Constantine, they were about ten minutes from the boat, having stopped to eat, and then they would begin the business of "fishing" for the truth. Translation: setting up Flores. She finished off a bite of food, listening to his plan to lure Carlos into the open and prove Flores to be innocent or guilty.

"It sounds dangerous," she stated, wiping sauce off her hand.

Crumbling a burrito wrapper, Constantine tossed it in the bag. "Less dangerous than going public at the trial without dealing with this."

Reluctantly, she agreed, wishing their fantasy hotel stay could have lasted a bit longer. There were no easy answers to any of this. No putting off reality.

She inhaled and exhaled. "Okay then. What do I do?"

"I shipped Flores a prepaid phone—"

"You're kidding! When? Won't they track the address you mailed it from?"

He gave her a reprimanding look. "You'll never learn to trust me, will you? I bought the phone on the road the first night. I tossed a few bills at the clerk, and he mailed it for me."

Tension rushed from her shoulders. "You really thought ahead."

"You learn to do that when you live fighting for your life. I know Flores has the phone because I called him."

"When?" she asked, surprised by this news.

He patted the car's dash. "While I was nabbing our ride. He thinks things between the two of us are cool."

"But that's not the case." As much as he wanted to defend Flores, she'd seen the darkness in his eyes when the man's name came up, seen the doubt.

A muscle in his jaw jumped, his teeth clenched. "We'll know soon enough." He seemed to take stock of his emotions and, adopting a more businesslike, rather than bitter, tone, he said, "Here's how this will play out.

I'll call Flores and tell him I need cash, that I can't get to my funds, but that I'll get back to him with the drop location. As soon as I hang up, you call him. Tell him I'm in a convenience store and you grabbed the phone. You're scared. Tell him I'm on a vengeance trip, hunting Carlos, planning to kill him. Tell him you need help, and then give him the boat's location."

She considered the plan. "You think he'll send Carlos?"

"If he's on their side, yes."

"And then we bust Flores and arrest Carlos."

"Right." He closed his eyes and took a deep breath before slowly letting it push past his lips. He was avoiding eye contact. What else was he avoiding? The truth? She didn't want to believe that.

True, they'd only spent a short while together, but she liked to think they'd come to an understanding. They'd talked about personal things, done personal things. Heck, she'd told him details she never would have told the man she'd called her husband. About her father, her mother, even her self-hatred over the past.

She touched his arm. "You *are* going to arrest him, right? Or is there more truth than fiction to the story I'm feeding Flores?"

Still, he didn't look at her. His lips thinned and tension crackled in the air. Finally, his lashes lifted and he fixed her in a level stare. "I'll try, Nicole, but if it comes down to him escaping…he won't be escaping. I won't let him walk away."

Nicole felt as if she'd been punched in the stomach. She'd asked for the truth, and he'd given it to her. Now she wasn't so sure that was a good thing. She didn't want to be faced with answering questions later and having to choose Constantine over the truth.

When she said nothing, he opened the compartment between the seats and pulled out a phone. He dialed Flores's number to set up Flores for Nicole's call. When the call ended, Constantine offered the phone to Nicole.

She reached for it, but he didn't let it go. "Carlos will hunt us down and kill us, Nicole. He can't go free or we'll never be free." He released his grip on the phone.

Didn't he see? If she had any more blood on her hands, she wouldn't be free, either.

But she didn't say that. She turned away from him and faced forward. "What's the number?"

He didn't immediately respond, the heaviness of his stare bearing down on her with leaden intensity. "Nicole—"

Shoving her hair behind her ears, she cast him a sideways look. "What's the number?" If he dared tell her what to say again, she'd quit the whole scheme.

He gave her the number and zipped his lips. Smart man. She dialed and did her best job of acting panicked.

Flores questioned her, a hint of suspicion in his voice. "How did you get this number?"

"I heard him call you. He went into a quick stop and left the phone. I thumbed through the numbers." She hesitated. "Oh, he's coming back. Pier thirty-nine. A boat called *Adiós*. We're only about an hour away." She disconnected and let out a breath before handing the phone to Constantine. "Now what?"

He gave her a steady look. "You did good."

She bit back an urge to ask why he would think she would do otherwise. "Now what?"

He shifted in his seat and started the engine. "Now we go get those supplies, find a place to wait, and see who shows up."

15

IN THE SHORT DRIVE to the pier, they didn't speak. Constantine didn't know why he'd tried to explain himself to Nicole. She didn't like lies, and it wasn't his problem if she couldn't deal with the truth. So why did it feel like his problem? He quickly whipped the car into a parking spot that offered a view of the boat. It also left them exposed. Not that he had options.

The parking garage across from the pier had been closed because of the approaching storm, and he didn't have time to waste finding another space. Carlos would be close by; he operated out of Padre. Exactly why they'd come here in the first place. Carlos would never expect him on his home turf.

Constantine debated. Leave Nicole in the car or bring her with him? A debate that ended when he admitted he couldn't risk her being in danger without him by her side.

He reached over Nicole, grinding his teeth against the sweetness of those barely parted thighs. Opening the glove compartment, he pulled out a gun, slammed the compartment shut and handed the weapon to Nicole.

"Where am I supposed to hide this?" she asked, referring to her thin shorts and T-shirt.

Good point. When all else fails, improvise. He

grabbed the Taco Bell bag and dumped the contents. "Use this."

Her eyes widened in disbelief, but she took the bag. "A purse would be so much better." Her gaze skimmed his shorts. "What about you?"

"Bag in the back," he commented. "I want in and out of the boat in no more than ten minutes."

She nodded. "Got it. I was thinking. How are you so certain that Carlos himself will be here today? Couldn't Flores send someone else? Maybe Carlos isn't near enough to get here in time?"

The question he'd expected her to ask before now. She wouldn't like the answer. "I'm a gambler, remember?"

"And I'm not a dope, remember?"

Inwardly, he smiled. Damn, she was tough. "He'll be in the area."

A frown on her face, she turned to him. "How would you know that for certain?"

"I spent three years in his world. I know how to bait Carlos."

He cut off further conversation, reaching for his door. "We're wasting valuable time that could get us killed. Let's get this done and over with. Stay close to me." He hesitated. "I don't want you in the open any longer than needed. Count to ten once my door shuts. That'll give me time to grab my bag."

Without waiting for her answer, he stepped out of the car, the wind gusting at him with the intensity that would throw Nicole around like a feather. Damn it. He hated exposing her to danger of any type, but the idea of letting her out of his sight twisted his gut in knots. Not a feeling he cared to analyze right now, either.

Instead, he focused on the horizon, where a dark wall of clouds was looming.

He squatted down beside the seat, eyes level with Nicole's. "Forget counting. Wait on me. I'll come get you. And forget the gun. The wind is too strong for you to try to hold on to it, let alone fire."

A grim expression on her face told of her understanding, so he pushed to his feet, slammed the door shut and scanned. By the time he retrieved the bag from the backseat, he'd inventoried the area. A total of five cars in the parking lot. To his right, a patrolman, a Padre Island police officer, talked in animated fashion to a young couple taking pictures, obviously trying to run them off. On the dock, two men worked to secure a boat, and Constantine frowned. The storm was ready to swallow them whole as it was.

He rounded the rear of the vehicle to help Nicole. Obviously aware of his location, she shoved open her door a second before he would have reached for it.

The minute she stood up, her hair blew in wild array around her face, and Constantine wished she had it pulled back as he did. She needed a clear view of what might be coming at her from both Mother Nature and man.

"We need to get out of here!" she hollered.

"Not without those supplies," he said, offering her his arm.

She slipped her arm under his elbow, not bothering to argue further. "You mean not before we get Carlos."

He planned to ignore her comment. She seemed to read his mind, refusing to be dismissed. She squeezed his arm and shouted into the howl of the wind. "I want him, too!"

Acceptance of his agenda shouldn't have been important, but somehow it was. Somehow, she'd known he needed to hear those words.

His hand closed over hers, silent appreciation of what she'd said, but he had to stay focused. Time was critical and so were the instructions he had given her. They needed to move. He pulled her forward, and they managed all of one step before a wind gust slammed into them. Constantine muscled up against the impact, and Nicole clung to him to keep from stumbling, yelling something he couldn't understand. He pulled her forward, fighting through the weather to get those supplies before Carlos arrived. He had a safe on the boat with enough cash to last a month. He figured it wouldn't be necessary. A month from now, she would be home, the trial complete. Or so he hoped.

Watching for trouble, holding on to Nicole and fighting the weather, Constantine charged toward the boat. As they walked down the dock ramps, water splashed and it didn't take long for them to be drenched.

Constantine climbed onto the wildly rocking deck of the *Adiós* and deposited his bag on the floor, before grabbing Nicole and pulling her to safety. Once he was certain she had a grip and steady footing, he retrieved his bag and guided her down a small staircase into the cabin.

Now, he had to fetch the money and supplies and get the heck out of Dodge. Easy. Fast. Yeah, right. Every nerve ending in his body tingled.

This juiced-up, edgy feeling was more than readiness; it was his inner alarm for trouble—the one that had kept him alive many a time. And he didn't plan to make this time any different.

THE BOAT CREAKED from side to side, forcing Nicole to cling to the wall. Constantine moved aside a picture and opened a safe, removing a smaller safe, which he shoved into his bag.

The inside of the boat was small and Nicole didn't like it. But she didn't have time to panic. Not now. Nicole inhaled; the cabin smelled warm and masculine like Constantine. The scent comforted and she focused on that feeling. He'd spent time here. This was his boat. "Is this your home?"

"Buying a boat had advantages. Mobility for one. And for a few bucks a year, I pay someone to do general maintenance."

If Constantine had been anyone else, Nicole would have asked if the person maintaining the boat could betray him. But she knew very well that Constantine would never let that person know his real identity. Not when she suspected this boat was his escape route in times of trouble.

He opened a cabinet and pulled out a couple of telephones and various other items that went into the bag. Ammunition, she thought. "The boat allows me to disappear if I need to," he commented, confirming what she'd been thinking. More times than not, he did that—finished her thought, answered a silent question. After a few days, she almost expected as much. He continued, "And it would have been the perfect escape if not for this storm." Moving to a closet, he pulled a rain slicker off a hanger. "Catch." He tossed it to her.

She snagged the shiny black jacket, noting the puddle of water around her feet. The ocean had drenched them far worse than the rain in the woods. At this rate, she would end up permanently shivering.

While she slid the oversize jacket into place, and rolled the sleeves up so they were manageable, Constantine strapped a shoulder holster around his body and shoved a Glock inside. He covered the weapon with a rain slicker matching the one she now wore.

Next thing she knew he was by her side, crisscrossing a small satchel over her chest and shoulder. He patted the bag. "Now you need a gun. Don't try to fire in this wind unless you absolutely have to."

"Like I would fire otherwise."

Displeasure flitted across his features. "I know how big you are on justice and doing the right thing. But out here in the field, a willingness to use your weapon can save your life."

She would have been irritated about being lectured to on other occasions, but this time, the warning settled hard in her stomach. She could do this, she reminded herself. She was tough.

Resolve taking root, Nicole drew herself upright despite the roughness of the boat's movement. "I know. I'm no fool. I'll shoot if I have to. I think I've proven that."

"I know you aren't a fool," he said, his taut voice taking a gentler note. "But shooting tires and shooting a person aren't the same. It can be hard for the most experienced people to pull the trigger. You can't hesitate."

Right again, of course, and she knew it. "I'll shoot if I have to."

He studied her a moment longer and inclined his head, apparently satisfied with her reply and already back in action mode. Grabbing his bag, he pointed to the stairs. "Let's roll. I'll go first to be sure we're clear."

A few seconds later, they were back outside, and the

weather had worsened. The rain had started, and the wind was even stronger than before. Constantine jumped to the docks and offered Nicole his hand, which she tried to accept, but with the wobble beneath her feet she couldn't quite connect with his palm.

Suddenly a scream ripped through the air, and Constantine retracted his hand, reaching for his gun. Nicole grabbed the boat railing with a solid grip.

More screams, this time more intelligible. "Help! Help!"

Nicole's adrenaline spiked into overdrive, her eyes searching in desperation for the source of the cries. Her gaze scanned the area, spotting a woman on the deck of a boat, several spots down from the *Adiós*. The woman was at the railing, struggling with a life preserver, steadying herself a second before she shoved it over the edge.

Hair blew in Nicole's eyes, slapping at her cheeks and brow, as she tried to see the reason for the woman's fear. She leaned down, looking beneath a sail and honed in on the water, where she saw a man struggling against the rough waves.

Oh, God. He was going to drown. She turned to Constantine and screamed his name, pointing out what she'd seen. He maneuvered closer, ducking down for a visual. A curse followed. Obviously he had managed to see what she did, his expression grim. He seemed to weigh his options, before turning to Nicole and reaching for her. "Come on."

Before Nicole could catch her breath, he had a hold of her and she was lifted from the boat onto the dock. The instant her feet hit the ground, he had her hand, and they were running, water and wind smacking them hard.

Seconds later, Nicole and Constantine climbed onto

the woman's boat. She ran at them, frantically pleading, "Save him! Please save my husband."

Constantine handed Nicole his gun, dropping his bag on the ground.

Fear squeezed her heart. The water was insanely dangerous, the wrath of Mother Nature much worse than Carlos and Alvarez put together. "You stay alive, damn it!" she shouted, her gut churning much like the ocean.

He didn't answer. She wasn't even sure he heard her. Already, he was diving over the side of the boat. She faced the sobbing woman and asked, "Do you have a phone? Have you called 911?"

"No, yes, I…have a phone."

"Use it! Call! Call now! And go get help." Nicole ran to the ledge to check for a ladder. Thankfully, the woman had, indeed, extended a rope ladder over the side.

Preparing to help if needed, she dropped Constantine's gun and holster next to the bag that he'd left on the deck. She returned to the railing, gulping water as rain slammed into her face. Coughing, she swiped at her eyes, desperately searching for Constantine. The minute she spotted him swimming through the salty turbulence, she breathed a bit easier. He was moving; he was visible. And yes! He had the drowning man in his grasp. She watched as he swam toward them, pulling the man with him through the powerful waves.

How long Nicole stood there, terrified for Constantine, watching him struggle, she didn't know, but it felt like a lifetime before he finally arrived at the edge of the boat, the man still in his grip. Thankfully, the woman showed up with help. Nicole turned to find two men wearing uniforms of some sort—beach patrol, she thought.

The two men started to lift the drowning man from the water, which meant Constantine could follow. With the woman's husband safely on board, stretched out and unconscious, one of the patrolmen dropped to his knees and appeared ready to start CPR. The other cop was leaning over the side of the boat trying to help Constantine.

Nicole ran to the edge, fearful, wondering why Constantine hadn't shown himself. Her heart felt as if it would explode at what she saw. Somehow, Constantine had been swept away from the boat by the rough waters. She watched as he grabbed the life preserver, and she let out a sigh of relief.

She turned to check on everyone else, only to find an order barked in her direction. "Go flag the ambulance!" The shout came from the man doing CPR. Nicole blinked. Was he talking to her? She glanced at the wife, who was crumpled to the ground next to her unmoving husband. Nicole's gaze flickered to the victim; his face appeared somewhat bluish and she understood why the woman was crying. Her husband was dying. Nicole had to do something.

She started running, or rather stumbling, across the deck toward the dock. Her heart jackknifed in her chest. Constantine would not like what she was doing. She didn't like it herself. Carlos was coming. She jumped off the boat to the wooden walkway, landing on her feet, and then darted toward the parking lot. Her mind went back to the silent threat. Carlos. Coming soon. How much time had passed? Thirty minutes? Forty?

It didn't matter, she told herself. She had to do this. But fear gripped her as she had the thought; she realized she was creating more danger for these people. Everyone on that boat was in danger—they'd be in danger because they were near her and Constantine.

She should turn back. A dim eeriness had claimed what was daylight only an hour before, which added to the growing unease rattling her nerves. By the time she'd made it to the parking lot, she was nervous, and had convinced herself she'd made the wrong move. About to abandon her efforts, she was waylaid by flashing red lights that blasted through the haze of the storm.

Charging toward the ambulance, determined to get their attention and get back to the boat, Nicole felt hope form that all of this would work out. After all, the ambulance was here. That was something. She clung to that little bit of good news.

The emergency crew, which consisted of two men, pulled to a stop beside her and she directed them where to go. And then she took off running toward the boat, not allowing them time to respond, ignoring their shouts behind her.

Hope filled her. She'd pulled off helping that man without getting herself killed. Hope that quickly faded as she found a man standing in front of the walkway that led to the docks. Stocky, with an air of menace clinging to him. Nicole had no doubt who she faced. *Carlos*.

16

NICOLE'S SURVIVAL INSTINCTS kicked in at the sight of Carlos in her path. She turned and cut a sharp left off the path she was on, and started running toward the car from another angle—leading Carlos away from the unsuspecting emergency crew, fearful for their safety. A gunshot sounded behind her, a blast that cut through the fierceness of the wind with a vicious roar. Nicole nearly jumped out of her skin, cringing in preparation for pain that never came. Somehow she kept running. Another shot was fired. No, two. Two shots.

She took a sharp left, toward their parked car. Carlos would follow her, then no one else had to die. She reminded herself she had a gun in the car. Now she had to focus on running, on getting to shelter so she could use it.

The car came into view and she pushed through the sting in her legs, against the power of the wind, running faster, harder. She could use the car for a shield, and then she'd pull her gun. Constantine was wrong to doubt her willingness to shoot. She'd shoot and she'd survive.

She approached the car and to her amazement, and relief, Constantine was right behind her. He charged at her, grabbed her arm and dragged her to a squat out of sight, beside the driver's door.

He held her shoulders, inspecting her for injuries. "You're okay?"

She blinked at him, rain rolling over her hair and lashes. They were both completely, utterly soaked.

"Nicole! Are you okay?"

"Yes." The one word was barely audible. Her teeth were chattering, but she wasn't cold. Reality slipped back into her mind. "It was Carlos! Where did he go?" She grabbed his forearms where he held her. "Where? Where is he?"

"Close. Too damn close. I got a shot off at him, but I missed. He slipped out of sight. But he's here."

"And so are a lot of innocent people."

His jaw flexed. "I know that all too well." He fixed her in a reprimanding look. "You shouldn't have left. You could have been killed."

"I—"

He cut her off. "Now isn't the time. Stay down."

Constantine started to stand, but stilled when one of the police officers from the boat appeared, his firearm drawn.

"Drop your weapon!" the man ordered.

"Easy now, kid," Constantine said. "I'm FBI. Call it in on—"

"Shut up! My partner is dead. I don't give a damn if you're the Lone Ranger."

Nicole's heart sank. Oh, God. "He didn't kill your partner. He's FBI. It was—"

"Shut up!" the kid yelled again and focused on Constantine. "Drop the gun."

Constantine held his gun by his side, showing no signs of throwing it away. "That man who killed your partner is after us. Throwing down my weapon would be a death sentence."

"Please," Nicole added, "let him do his job. Before it's too late."

The patrolman shifted his gaze between them and then fixed on Constantine again. "I'll do it when the gun is on the ground."

The muffled sound of a motorcycle broke through the noise of the storm, and Constantine stiffened beside her. "That would be the man who killed your partner, and now he plans to kill us." The sound grew louder. "Look, kid," Constantine said, his tone like hard steel, "I'm losing my patience with you. You're impeding an FBI operation." He raised his voice. "If you don't stop aiming your weapon at me in about two seconds—"

Abruptly, he stopped talking. The sound of a motorcycle was fast approaching. "Get down!"

Nicole hit the ground. The patrolman didn't. Constantine launched himself at the kid and took him to the pavement, smack in the center of a puddle that splashed mud all over. And not a second before a spray of bullets hit the car. Nicole covered her head, her heart thundering along with the motorcycle engine as it sped by.

The minute the sound of the bike faded, Constantine shoved off the patrolman and stood up. Nicole followed his lead and did the same, moving to Constantine's side, the place he'd once again proven to be the safest.

The patrolman scrambled to his feet, his expression flustered and confused. Constantine looked at the man, his face full of disgust. "Call for backup," he ordered as he returned his weapon to the holster. Carlos had to have gone. How he knew this, Nicole wasn't sure, but she was learning not to doubt him. Not when it came to his job.

Constantine wasn't done with the patrolman. Not by a long shot. "When you call for that backup, tell them you just let Carlos Menchaca get away." He bent down and retrieved the kid's weapon from the puddle and let it dangle from his finger. The kid grabbed it.

Constantine motioned toward the car, and she didn't argue. She wanted out of there. Her life had become hell.

Once they were in the car, she was relieved to see the bag of supplies in the backseat. Constantine must have remembered to bring them. He started the engine and squealed out of the driveway. A second later, he grabbed the phone that was stuffed in the compartment between the seats and dialed. "Give me Agent Nelson. Tell him Agent Vega is on the phone."

Nicole gaped at that, shocked he trusted anyone at this point, especially Nelson after the way he'd reacted to his involvement. "Vega here," he said to the receiver, she assumed to Nelson. "Menchaca is in Padre, near pier thirty-nine. He killed a cop, tried to take us out, too." He listened a minute as they pulled up behind a line of traffic at a standstill. "Local police have their hands full with the storm."

Constantine did some more listening, and offered a few short, clipped words in reply. Then, he dropped his bomb on Nelson. "Flores is dirty." He went on to describe the way they had set him up and ended with, "I suggest you deal with him before I get back." Silence, listening, then he said, "And, Nelson. This doesn't mean I trust you. It simply means you're all I got right now. I'll be in contact soon."

He hung up. Neither Nicole nor Constantine spoke, the tension in the car as thick as the storm surrounding them. Nicole wanted to lie back and think, to calm the chaos going on in her brain. But that would have been too easy. She should have known there would have been complications to come. Without warning, Constantine whipped the car into a hotel parking lot, drove to the rear and shut off the ignition.

"Carlos knows this car. We have to switch vehicles. Wait here." Right. No keys to leave since it was hot-wired. His exit came with obvious effort, as he fought a gust of wind and lots of water.

So Nicole waited. Waited while he stole another car. And though she knew the government would cover the expense, it was still stealing. She tried not to think of a family in need, reminding herself they could rent a car. That she and Constantine would be dead without escape. They had no help. Worse, she wanted another car. She wanted to feel safe. If she kept at this a few more days, lived in Constantine's world, would she justify vigilante acts to save lives, too?

As she'd feared, the right circumstances, the right person—aka Constantine—and she was back to her old self. Or getting there. Suddenly, she didn't want to claim her darker side. She wanted to blame someone. Anger and frustration over all of that twisted inside her.

The back door opened, more wind, more rain. Constantine grabbed the supplies. "We're a go."

Steeling herself for the weather, Nicole reached for the door and pushed it open. Seconds later, she was inside a four-door sedan, a Mercury maybe, basically a perfect match for the car they'd left behind—wet and stolen.

"Where are we going?"

"Houston. They'll expect us to go farther. We won't."

She didn't comment. Houston. Dallas. Canada. All

that mattered was that she got back to Austin, alive and ready for trial. Which would be delayed at this point, but she hoped not too long. Too many things could go wrong with a long delay.

In a matter of minutes, Constantine maneuvered them onto the highway, and into a traffic jam. Great. Trapped in a car, feeling edgy, in a traffic jam. In a storm. If that didn't trigger her claustrophobia, she didn't know what would.

She inhaled and let out a breath, focusing on anything but the small space, her gaze sliding to his profile. A strong profile, a grim set to his jaw. A stubborn, hard-ass man. Her anger hadn't faded. "You shouldn't have been so rough on that kid."

He glanced at her, his brows set in a straight line. "I saved his life." Constantine's voice was low, unaffected by her attack.

"Today," she countered. "What about how it affects him? How it will impact his ability to do his job?"

A sound of disbelief slid from his lips. "I can't believe you're comparing him to either of us. And don't deny you are because I know better. The impact of my words on that kid doesn't even begin to compare to what you and I have been through to get where we are now. In fact, what happened to him today might well save his life, and other lives, many times over. He won't ever be as careless as he was today."

"He lost his partner. That's the part you seem to be forgetting."

"And he acted irrationally and emotionally, ignoring his training. A good way to get others killed. We could have helped him get the man who killed his partner. Instead, Carlos is free, and he's going to keep coming.

For me. For you. For anyone we care about. So did you think I was going to give him a lollipop and thank him for screwing us?"

She took those harsh words with a stunned blast and fell back in her seat, not even aware she had been sitting up in confrontation mode. Realization dawning, she said, "I thought this was about justice and helping people. Why does it feel like I'm hurting more than I'm helping right now?" Her lashes shut, blocking out nothing, when she wanted to block out everything—at least for a few minutes.

Silence followed before he replied, "You are helping, Nicole. But there is no such thing as that easy black-and-white line that you want to believe exists. Fighting to find that safe middle wears on a person."

She turned to him, her lashes lifted. "Wears on you?"

"Hell, yes. That's why I'm getting out. I'm done and gone after this, and never looking back."

A hint of pain tinged his voice. She'd almost forgotten. "I'm sorry about Flores."

He shrugged, but he didn't look at her. "It's done. He's done. That's what counts."

"Do you want to know why he did it?"

"Nope," he said, glancing at her. "He was part of an attempt on our lives. He couldn't give me a reason that would matter. They'll suspend him and hold him for questioning until we get back and then I'll give them what they need to lock him away for good."

She drew a long, hard breath. This had hurt him. Betrayal hurt. If he wasn't ready to leave his job before this, she imagined that Flores had sealed the deal. Still… "You really think you can simply shut off this world. Forget this part of your life?"

He answered quickly, as if he'd given the question a lot of consideration before she'd asked it. "For a while. Then, I'll see where to go from there. I haven't had time to spend my money so I invested it. I have time to decide. Private hire work is an option. It would be nice to choose my own battles."

She turned away from him, lost in her own thoughts. *Choose my own battles.* She figured she'd done that by joining the U.S. Attorney's office. Now, she wasn't so sure. The battles sure seemed to be picking her these days. The internal emotional battle to find her place— the reason she'd made a career change—still existed, never letting her find peace.

Nicole had opened this conversation with Constantine looking to blame him for how out of control she felt. But the truth was, he not only wasn't to blame, his words, his actions, made sense to her. *He* made sense to her. He'd saved lives today, acted bravely. He was a hero. A hero who didn't always play by the rules, but he always had good intentions.

She admired him. She desired him. She felt safer with him near. And she feared him. Or maybe she feared herself and simply hated him for making her look deep enough to know it.

Once again, she came to the conclusion he always led her to—Constantine was dangerous. And that danger, she feared, was becoming an addiction she wondered if she would ever recover from.

17

CONSTANTINE HAD BARELY spoken to Nicole during the grueling hours in traffic, making the short trip to Houston progress far too slowly. But then, that was the idea. He wanted to get lost in the midst of the evacuation chaos. But along the way, he got lost in his own internal struggles. Now, walking down the hall of the high-end, high-security, downtown hotel toward their room, Nicole by his side, Constantine warned himself to dump the emotional garbage. It was dangerous, deadly, distracting.

The truth was, being betrayed by Flores had bitten him pretty hard, but it was nothing in comparison to when he'd climbed up to the deck of that boat and discovered Nicole was missing. That moment had pierced him with sheer terror. A feeling he'd had only once before—when he got the call about his brother.

Nicole had gotten under his skin, and apparently past an emotional barrier that he didn't know could be penetrated. He was pissed at her for running off, at himself for becoming susceptible to Nicole. People around him had short life spans. It was the curse of his world.

For the second time in an hour, Constantine shoved open the door to their room. "You're sure you have everything?" he asked, dropping a handful of bags on the floor and then locking up. They'd checked in under an alias, surveyed the room and then left to stock up heavily on items they might need for their extended stay. "We can't leave for anything. And I can't stress that enough. It's dangerous. We slid in here as part of the background to the craziness of the storm. Once that calms, we'll get more attention. We're here to stay."

Nicole sat down on the bed, settling several large Macy's bags on the mattress beside her. She'd been tentative with him the entire shopping spree, no doubt because of his foul mood, or perhaps she was still angry over how he'd treated that patrolman back in Padre.

"I have everything I need," she confirmed. "And thank you." She hesitated and repeated a question she'd asked several times before. "You're sure the department will reimburse you, right?"

If he answered truthfully, no. The department only covered basics, but he'd be damned if he'd admit that. Convincing her to shop from his wallet had taken heavy prodding. He expected the claustrophobia would kick in after two days of staying in the room, so having some of her personal comforts would help. Even people without a phobia got restless fast.

"I'm sure," he said, walking to the midsize fridge in the corner to unload a few items. He could feel her watching him, feel the heaviness of her stare.

They might be tense, but they were alone in a hotel room, two people who had more than their share of desire for one another. A sizzle of sexual energy crackled in the air. But then, their chemistry was a given at that point.

Nicole's soft laugh laced the air, a hint of nervousness in the sound, as if she were responding to the mixed array of emotional baggage between them and was as confused by it as he was.

"Thanks to the storm," she commented, toeing off her stained tennis shoes, "today was probably the only time in my life I could get away with walking into Macy's looking like a female mud wrestler."

Constantine deposited several cans of Diet Sprite in the fridge—Nicole's "favorite drink." "For all the trouble that storm caused us, it certainly helped us in other ways."

He looked up to find Nicole unpacking their purchases, his gaze lingering on her graceful movements, her delicate hands reminding him of how amazing her touch felt. He didn't understand—when had looking at a woman's hands turned him on?

Inwardly, he shook himself, and went back to packing the fridge, but his mind played with the experience of watching her shop, which had been rather enlightening. All her products, her choices, had told a lot about Nicole. She had a thing for a perfume called "Passion" and apparently anything else sold at the Estée Lauder cosmetic counter. She liked red and pink silk pajamas, which he looked forward to seeing her in…and out of. At his prodding, she'd picked out a couple of work suits for the first few days of the trial; they were preparing to stay in hiding as long as possible. Her contrasting choices of sexy sleepwear and conservative work attire had intrigued him. She was the perfect woman. He paused in the act of putting orange juice away, wondering where that thought had come from.

Before he could venture further, Nicole drew him into conversation. "I really don't know how you stand always being undercover. I need my safe haven, my space that I escape to."

Which was why he'd made sure she'd purchased items she would use at home, hoping to give her a sense of control. "When you're deep undercover, you take on a persona that feels like it's you. If you don't, you won't survive."

She stopped what she was doing and stared at him. "Sounds like a hard way to live."

"After a while, the act becomes second nature. We can train ourselves to step out of our comfort zones." Just as she had. The writing was on the wall. She wanted to be the staunch federal prosecutor, but there were parts of that role she struggled to embrace. "But I suspect you know that." He didn't give her time to respond, not wanting to make her defensive, regretting he'd even spoken the words. They'd had enough tension during the long ride. He pushed to his feet. "You can have the shower first."

"That sounds good." She glanced at the clock. "I am supposed to call Dean in an hour regarding that motion to suppress your testimony by the defense."

"Which you're sure they won't get."

She scoffed, pushing off the bed with a bag in hand. "About as good a chance as snow in mid-July."

Her words held spunk; her mood seemed to lift as her zeal for victory appeared to take hold. Clearly, she enjoyed the battle, and enjoyed winning her cases. But then, it was clear that the lines they had drawn in order to reach success were the same lines that were creating all her conflict. They both lived the conflicting messages their legal system elicited, both struggled with them. But each of them had taken a different path to deal with the obstacles they faced from that system. She'd gone to one side of the line, he to the other. Ironically, neither of them liked the result.

Could there be two people so similar and so different in this world?

He watched her sashay past him, heading to the bathroom. His gaze dropped, lingered, riveted on her perfect ass, his groin tightening as he thought of all the things he was going to do to her there, in that room. They'd better enjoy what time they had.

Because when they left that room, there would be a tough trial and tough decisions. Like twenty-four-hour security for Nicole. Not something he planned to bring up until he had to.

Meanwhile, he'd protect her and then get the hell out of her life, so she could avoid the danger that always affected those around him. Which meant they should now burn out the chemistry they shared. And something told him that was going to require a lot of time in bed.

HEAVEN. HER BATH had been heaven.

Nicole slipped into the pink velour sweatpants and matching T-shirt she'd bought, and inhaled the scent of her favorite bubble bath still floating in the air. She'd bought a few bras, but she didn't bother putting one on, nor did she bother with panties—panty lines were something she could do without.

Spraying on some perfume, Nicole felt nearly herself again. She didn't consider herself spoiled, by any means, but her little habits gave her a sense of pleasure she now realized should never be taken for granted. Next up, drying her hair, applying a little makeup. The idea of Constantine seeing her as a woman, not a mess, appealed far more than she cared to admit. Especially since they'd been anything but friendly the past few hours. Still, the attraction between them lingered, waiting for exploration as readily as a new day. No one resisted such an attraction in close quarters. Sex was a basic need, a need she'd long denied herself. Of all the things Constantine had awakened in her, her sexual appetite was top of the list.

She sighed and leaned on the sink, staring at her image. More than her sexuality had been reinvented since meeting Constantine. But then, she'd sensed he would do this to her. Sensed he was the catalyst that would create inevitable change in her life. Remembering the night she'd met him, she recalled the air of dangerous excitement he'd sparked in her. The way she'd known he would somehow make her look inside herself, force her to examine realities she wasn't sure she was willing to face. Deep down, she had known she'd been hiding from herself. Constantine had led her to a crossroads. When this experience ended, she would have to choose a direction for her life.

Would she fight to walk that narrow, perfect line or would she detour? More and more that line felt constraining, and hearing Constantine's opinions on things made her realize how not black-and-white life could be. But if she detoured from this path, where did that leave her? So what was she? Who was she? Unhappy, she thought. Miserable. Tired of being something she wasn't. That left her where? She had no idea. She wanted Alvarez behind bars and so did Constantine. That mutual desire and their shared attraction had melted away their black-and-white viewpoints. But had she lost herself to him? Lost everything she'd fought to achieve? Lost the moral fiber on which she'd based her past few years of living?

Her mind went back to seeing Carlos, to running for her life. Yes, she had hoped for Carlos's demise, for Constantine to kill him. Oh, God. She knew why she was drawn to Constantine. He was so like her that it was scary.

She squeezed her eyes shut. Her problem these past few years had been with the system. She'd changed sides but the battlefield was the same. Grabbing the hairbrush, she roughly pulled it through her hair. She couldn't do this now, couldn't think about this now. She had to be her best during this trial, to put Alvarez away for life.

But later, she had to face some life-changing decisions, and she had Constantine to thank for that. Part of her hated him for it, while the other part felt grateful.

She'd funnel those emotions into the only outlet she had…sex.

NICOLE ENTERED the bedroom to find Constantine lying on the bed watching the news, his head propped up against the headboard, long legs stretched out in front of him, shirt off. Her mouth went dry. She didn't hide her inspection.

He looked every bit the sexy stranger she had seen in that bar that first night and then some. Knowing he was a dangerous temptation had only served to enhance her desire for him, to solidify the dark danger of his allure. She stood, unmoving, staring at him, him staring at her. Awareness built like warmth turning to heat… ready to burst into flames.

"Feel better?" he asked, his dark eyes mesmerizing in their directness. His voice had that lusty, provocative tone he used when they were intimate.

"Oh, yes. I feel much better," she said, walking toward the bed and sitting down on the end of the mattress. "I need to call Dean."

He grabbed the phone off the nightstand and handed it to her. "I like the outfit."

She took the phone, realizing his gaze had settled below her chin. Her nipples tightened and peaked, the heaviness of his attention creating equal heaviness in her breasts. The effect was a rush of sensation in her core, between her thighs.

She put a finger under his chin and lifted his gaze to her eyes. "Go take a shower. I have to call Dean, and I can't do it with you looking at me like that."

A slow, mischievous smile slid onto his lips, lighting those dark eyes. Damn, he was hot when he smiled. He didn't do it enough. "You can join me when you finish."

"I already took a bath and you didn't join me," she reminded him.

"You didn't invite me."

"We were barely speaking. I didn't think you wanted to be invited."

"You thought wrong and the last time I checked, bathing doesn't require speaking."

She laughed. He kissed her, his tongue swooping past her lips with a soft caress she felt in every inch of her body. Too soon, his mouth was gone, his thumb lingering, sliding over her bottom lip. "It's an open invitation, talking optional." He left her wanting and wet, and headed to the bathroom. She wanted to follow, but she really had to call Dean.

The bathroom door shut and she climbed across the bed to lean against the headboard, dialing Dean's number. He picked up in one ring, obviously waiting for her call, and offered her good news—Constantine's testimony was a go.

"Excellent. He's a strong witness. His brother and father were both in law enforcement."

"I know," Dean said. "I had him investigated."

"That was fast," she said, pleased to hear there were no skeletons in Constantine's closet, but not surprised. He was pretty straightforward about who he was, the good and the bad.

"The FBI expected we'd want the information," Dean commented. "They handed his file over on a silver platter. He not only looks good on paper, he has the defense shaking in their shoes."

She frowned. "Exactly why Alvarez wants him dead."

"And you, too," he grimly added, his voice muffled by static on the line, probably from the storm. "Anything to delay the trial and come up with a loophole. Which brings me to some not-so-good news."

"Which would be?"

"I talked to your—" More static.

"What? Talked to who?"

"I talked to your sister today. Your father wants her home and at work. She wanted to know how sure I was she should stay gone."

Nicole sat up, her heart pounding like a drum against her chest. "You told her to stay away, right?"

"I did, but she is feeling pressured. Your father wants her at work. He assured her he has private security and that those security people have seen absolutely no signs of a threat. He says—"

"He has money to make. I know. Believe me, I know my father. Damn it!" She ran a hand through her hair. "Why is she so manipulated by him? Why does she want to be like him so badly? And why doesn't he see how dangerous this is?" She had practically forgotten Dean. "Is she still in Hawaii?"

The phone cut in and out. "Did you hear me?" Dean asked. "She's taking a flight home first thing in the morning."

"I have to go." She'd call him back later, to check on his wife. She dialed her sister's cell. The call dropped, no signal.

Pushing to her feet, Nicole moved to the window and dialed again. Still, no signal. Why did her father do these things? Did he love and care about anyone? Sometimes his wallet seemed his only love. Truthfully, he wasn't a nice person. He was about control. About career. There was a reason she didn't include him in her life. But she knew her sister wanted him there. Just as she once had. He had a way of manipulating you and stealing your self-worth—making it exist based on his approval.

Giving up on getting a signal for the cell phone, she headed to the door. Maybe near the elevator she could get a signal. She hesitated and rushed into the bathroom, calling to Constantine through the shower curtain. "I'll be right back. There's an emergency at home and I can't get cell reception."

He yanked the shower curtain back. "No. Wait on me."

"I can't. I'll be right back."

She heard him curse, but she didn't care. Her sister was all that mattered right then. She'd deal with his anger, if and when—she didn't care. It wasn't as if she were leaving the floor, or leaving without communicating. He'd understand when he heard it was about her sister. He had to understand.

THE HOTEL-ROOM DOOR closed about the time Constantine wrapped the tiny towel around his waist. Was she begging to get killed or what? It took him all of twenty seconds to find his gun and head for the door, having no qualms about leaving in a towel. The one second he hesitated could be the difference between life or death. But this was a hell of a way to stay under the radar.

After confirming the hall to be vacant, a small miracle considering how busy the hotel was, he flipped the lock around to keep the door from closing all the way. With long strides, he headed for the elevator, heart thundering in his chest, fear for her safety far more controlling than his professional standards should allow.

Rounding the corner, he found relief. Nicole was pacing, talking on the phone, a deep frown on her face. The minute she saw him, her eyes went wide, her gaze sweeping his half-naked body, spotting the gun in his hand. Her face went pale.

Her expression said she knew she'd pushed him too far, given him one too many scares that day. She knew she'd done this to him, pushed him over the edge. His patience officially snapped; his emotions were unrecognizable. He didn't like what he was feeling—hated it, in fact.

He charged at her and grabbed her hand. "Come with me now or I swear to God I will throw you over my shoulder and carry you."

A stunned look filled her face and she mumbled into

the phone, "I'll call you back, but don't get on that plane until I talk to you again." Constantine gave her a warning look and she quickly said, "I'll call back," and hit End. "Constantine—" The elevator dinged, and panic registered on her face.

"Yeah, I'm in a towel about to give a peep show." He started pulling her down the hall and mumbled under his breath, "Which I have you to thank for."

"Ouch," she complained behind him. "You're hurting me."

He knew damn well he wasn't hurting anything but her pride. And that was lucky for her, but then, he wasn't through yet. Using one foot, he kicked open the door, and then reached up and flipped the latch, pulling Nicole inside the room. He used his foot again to make sure the door shut behind him.

Nicole tugged on her arm, leaning away from him as if to leverage herself. "Let. Me. Go."

He did the opposite. He yanked her to him, anchoring her against his body, palm against her lower back. Her body, soft and curvy, pressed into his. He prayed for patience. *"Por, Dios, da me paciencia."*

Palms flat on his chest, she glared at him. "Stop cussing at me in Spanish! If you have something to say, then you can say it in English."

"I didn't curse you. I simply asked God to give me the patience to deal with you."

"What?" she roared back. "I'm the one who needs patience. You're being a complete jerk. My sister is leaving Hawaii in the morning. I have to stop her from boarding that plane."

"I asked you to wait long enough for me to get out of the shower. I've risked my life for you over and over, and you can't wait for me to get out of the shower before you make that phone call? A few seconds was too much to ask?" His chest lifted with a hard inhalation that he quickly expelled. "You're driving me to insanity, woman."

"And you're such a joy, let me tell you!"

He knew he was overreacting, but somehow, quite out of character, he couldn't stop himself from doing so. He started toward the bed, but she dug her heels in. He pulled her tight against his body again, more than a bit irritated, and completely out of patience, hands cupping her round ass as he lifted her from the ground.

The act put her flat against his body, and his cock flared to life, the towel barely clinging to his hips. Her breasts pressed into his bare chest. She wore no bra, and he could feel her nipples as surely as he could her ass in his hands. Inwardly he cursed his lack of control. The heat of anger began to merge with the raging call of desire.

"Put me down," she admonished near his ear. A plea slipped into her voice. "Stop acting like this. Stop being—"

Her sentence was cut short by her back hitting the mattress. Constantine straddled her hips, his hands going to her wrists, holding them above her head. She struggled for a good minute before stilling. There was no chance she could get free and she knew it. He was bigger and stronger, and just as determined to hold her down as she was to get up.

His face was close to hers, his gaze latching on to hers with purpose, letting her see deep into the depths of his stare, letting her see how far she'd pushed him.

Take a deep, hard look, sweetheart. See what you've

unleashed in me. See the stranger I don't even know as myself.

"Constantine," she whispered, soft desperation in her voice. But he was still too damn mad to back down, and she deserved to feel the brunt of it. But damn it, his gaze dropped to her mouth, to those full, perfect lips as they quivered. The desire to kiss her, hold her and touch her rose within him like a caged beast demanding freedom. He wanted to take her right now, to find his way inside her, to dispel all the emotion he felt, inside the warm, wet heat of her body.

But he also knew he needed space, needed to clear his head. Needed to stay mad and deal with the real safety issues. His towel slid from his hips; the will to get off Nicole and walk away slid with it.

_18_

CONSTANTINE WAS DESPERATE to resist claiming Nicole. But he kissed her, capturing her mouth with his, branding her lips with fiery need. Instantly, she submitted to him, and he silently reveled in the victory of her response.

But her submission was short-lived. Nicole tore her mouth from his, her hands pressing on his bare chest, her touch teasing him with the possibility of all the places they might travel. "No," she whispered, her words desperate, laden with desire. "I want you, but not like this. Not when you're angry for no reason."

He rested on his elbows, one on either side of her, and stared into her eyes. "You scared the hell out of me." His voice was husky, with a gravelly tone he barely recognized as his own.

Confusion flashed across her features. "I thought your job didn't allow for emotional responses. That sounds emotional to me. You told that patrolman—"

He'd come that far, he might as well go all the way. "You're not simply a part of my job, Nicole. Not anymore." His fingers brushed her cheek, tenderness welling inside him…tenderness driving him insane with unfamiliar feelings. He didn't want to care about her, but there seemed no way to hide, nowhere to run.

Sliding her small wrists above her head, he easily

enclosed them in one of his larger hands. Her chest rose and fell, drawing his eyes to her deliciously peaked nipples, his cock throbbing, demanding satisfaction. He searched her face for a reaction.

Heat and defiance glinted in her eyes. "Holding on to someone like this, who is claustrophobic, is a good way to see the claws come out," she warned.

He considered her words, his free hand sliding over her arms, her neck, her breasts. She sucked in a breath as he lightly tweaked her nipple through the thin material of her T-shirt. "I know you explored the kinky side of sex with your ex. You mean to tell me you were never tied up?"

"Never."

"You didn't trust him."

"What's that got to do with anything?"

"Handing over complete control requires trust." He molded her breast more fully to his palm, bringing his lips to hers.

"I trust you," she murmured against his mouth, opening to allow his tongue to delve in for a quick sensual stroke.

"You trust me to some degree, but not fully." He released her arms to make a point.

A flare of fire in her eyes turned to confusion and then disappeared behind a mask of seductive play. "And if I wanted to tie you up? Would you let me?"

"Trust is a two-way street, sweetheart. If you don't give it freely, you don't get it freely." His hand slid up her shirt. "Take this off."

"I trust you," she argued, pulling her shirt over her head.

He worked her pants down her hips and tossed them

aside. He spread her legs, running his palms up her toned calves, over her knees, and then settled his hands on her thighs. He inched her legs farther apart, and she willingly opened to him.

Yes. There was some trust—trust within limits. She no longer demanded complete control, no longer needed the edge of power to enjoy his pleasuring her.

He slid his finger along the center of her core, and she whimpered softly. "You're wet for me."

"Yes," came the barely there reply, her voice growing stronger as she added, "And I shouldn't be. Not after you acted like a caveman dragging me into the room like you did."

Ah, and there it was, a hint of vulnerability he'd seen in her during their lovemaking. The fear that she was giving him too much, not holding back enough. He settled his erection in the sweet heat of her core, determined to kiss away whatever emotion drove her to throw up a shield.

His hands slid to her face; the feel of her soft curves pressed into his body was heaven in the middle of all the hell. "It's okay to want me, you know."

Her bottom lip trembled. She started to speak. Stopped. Started again. "You were right." The confession came in a shaky voice, a rarity for her, he was certain. She continued, "You do scare me. You scare the hell out of me. You make me question all the things I thought I knew and understood. You make me want things I shouldn't want."

"And you," he proclaimed, offering his own confession, "make me question everything I thought I wanted."

Silence—intense, full of sexual energy and emotion—fell between them then, their eyes locked in a soul-deep stare. On some gut level, he knew meeting Nicole was life-changing. She had touched him on a level he'd never fully recover from.

They moved then, together—at the same moment. They were kissing, crazy hot kissing, lost in the passion, consumed by the complete utter need for one another. Nothing mattered but here and now. He had tried to sate his desire to touch her soft skin, inhale that soft feminine scent, but nothing worked. He simply couldn't get enough of her, and he wondered if he ever would. Doubted that he ever could. She moved with equal, frenzied need, pressing close, arching into him. She felt what he did. Felt the burn he couldn't escape.

He realized then that all the obstacles between them had disappeared. What was left sent him over the edge, outside of reality. There were a million reasons why anything real between them couldn't work. His life and her life conflicted in far too many ways. He couldn't have her. But he could have her tonight, these few weeks—a stolen piece of time.

He took her then, finding his way inside her body, thrusting his cock deep inside the wet heat of her core. She gasped and clung to him, her lips and teeth nipping at his shoulder with delicious results he felt from head to foot.

Driven to see the passion in her face as he made love to her, he leaned back, staring down at her. Her eyes were heavy-lidded, her mouth swollen from his kisses. Slowly, he teased them both as he pulled out all but the head of his erection. "Constantine," she pleaded.

A plea that reached deep inside him, demanding a response. He lunged into her then, burying himself to the hilt, pulling back and repeating the action. Her breasts bounced and she covered them with her hands, kneading.

He craved her taste, reveled in her beauty, her touch. Her hands slid from her breasts to his shoulders, his neck. He was pumping and rocking, her legs wrapped around his, her hips cradling his.

"More," she cried out. "More." But he wasn't sure how to fulfill her need, his need. Never in his life had he felt so lost in a woman, so impossibly in need of complete possession. That possession, however, that completeness, somehow lingered out of reach.

Long moments they pumped, together, then stilled, staring at one another, and he saw in her what he felt in himself. They were both confused by the array of emotions, of pleasures rushing through them.

Her hair was wild around her heart-shaped face, her lips parted, waiting for him. "Damn, you're beautiful," he murmured, his mouth lowering to claim hers, his hands reaching beneath her backside, pulling her tighter against him. He angled her hips as he pumped some more, and she took more…begged for more. Until finally, too soon, not soon enough, she shattered—tense for seconds before her body jerked into release.

He still rode her, watching her, enthralled by the sight of her coming. Holding himself back, he waited until he knew she was completely satisfied. When her body began to ease, then, and only then, did he begin to allow his own final pleasure to consume him. He shattered much as she had, shaking with the intensity, stars before his eyes.

When finally his muscles eased, his release complete, they collapsed together, his head buried in her neck. He was still semi-hard, the massive orgasm he'd spilled inside her nowhere near enough to satisfy him. He didn't want to let go of her; he thought maybe he'd roll her on top and do that all over again.

The tempting idea was ended by Nicole's panicky voice. "Oh, my sister. I have to stop her from getting on that plane."

He leaned up on his elbows. "We'll stop her." Reluctantly, he rolled off her and hunted down his towel before handing it to her. "Tell me what's going on."

Nicole explained the situation, and Constantine shook his head. "I know he's your father, Nicole, but—"

Lifting a staying hand, she cut him off. "I know. He doesn't act as if he is. The man had the nerve to tell Brenda I'm a coward for hiding, and that she shouldn't be one, too. Criminal law involves criminals, he told her. If she can't deal with those people without hiding, she doesn't belong in criminal law."

He didn't know what to say to such a blatant insult aimed at Nicole, and from her father to boot. "Your mother? What does she think of all of this? Isn't she worried?"

"My mother doesn't put a sentence together my father doesn't form. My father will convince her this is all melodrama. That he has security if my sister needs it. I just want her away, safe. At least until some of this heat calms."

He watched as Nicole climbed under the sheet and pulled it to her neck as if she sought the safety of a shield— beyond her mental barriers this time. Her parents' attitude blew him away. Death might have claimed his family, but they'd all loved him, and he, them. She had no one but her sister, it seemed. Which offered yet another explanation— why she'd run out into that hall without waiting for him.

"I'll handle this," he told her, determined to make this go away for her. He reached for the phone and punched Redial, hoping for a signal, and finding one.

"Who are you calling?"

"Your sister," he said.

Her eyes went wide, but before she could object, Brenda answered. "Nicole! Is that you? Are you okay?"

"Nicole is fine," he replied. "She's right here beside me. Brenda, this is Agent Constantine Vega."

"What's wrong?" Brenda demanded. "Are you sure Nicole is safe?"

"Yes, she's safe." He didn't look at Nicole because he was about to share some harsh words with her sister. "Your safety is the concern, and I'm not going to mince words here. The man hunting your sister means to kill her. He'll use anyone he can to get to her, but he prefers pretty women as targets. He'll do his homework. Probably already has. He knows how important you are to Nicole. If he gets his hands on you, he'll be brutal because he enjoys pain. He'll enjoy your pain. *Stay where you are.*"

Silence. "I don't know what to do. My father says—"

"We aren't dealing with your basic criminal type here. Believe me, far worse. Does your father want the death of both his daughters on his conscience?"

More silence. "How is Nicole?"

Constantine glanced at Nicole for the first time since the call started. Her knees were drawn to her chest, sheet clutched in her fist, apprehension etching her features.

"She's beyond worried for you. If you go home, I'll have to tie her down to keep her here." Nicole's eyes went huge and he winked.

"I know who you are. She told me. You're the man from the bar."

He didn't like that statement. "Stay where you are, Brenda."

She hesitated. "I'm going to catch all kinds of heck for this, but I'll stay. Can I talk to Nicole?"

"Yes." He hesitated, though, eventually handing the phone to Nicole.

Nicole talked to her sister for a minute and hung up. "Thank you," she said. "Thank you so very much."

He tugged the sheet away from her and pulled her into his arms. "Thank me in that shower I never finished. After that, I am fairly confident I'll need to make love to you again."

He scooped her up. Standing with her in his arms, he carried her to the bathroom, a heated image playing in his head of what he planned to do to her once he got her there.

HOURS LATER, Nicole woke, lying on her stomach. The room was dark, night having fallen during their sleep. She smiled to herself. Constantine's hand was on her bare butt. Definitely a butt man.

She sighed softly, thinking of the hours of lovemaking they'd shared. *Lovemaking.* His word, not hers. But what had happened between them had been far more fulfilling, far more potent than any sex she'd experienced before him. Indeed, *lovemaking.* What she'd had with her ex had been pure sex. This…this experience with Constantine ran deeper than simple pleasures of the body. It drew her into a mind-set where the rest of the world faded into a place she shared with only one other—with Constantine.

Her mind traveled to his comments about trust. She

did trust him. What he had done with her sister blew her away. He'd come through for her, protected Brenda and done so for her. Yes. She trusted him. Mostly. With her life. But with her heart? That thought brought her back to her fears.

He scared her. No. Her reaction to him scared her. He reached inside her and saw everything she would hide from another. She didn't want to be hurt. Letting him get too close would only make saying goodbye harder. He was wrong for her, but he felt so right. The questions he made her ask of herself were difficult, but somehow necessary.

Here in Constantine's arms, she had found a different sort of comfort. Yet something inside her screamed to run from this feeling, to push him away. He'd leave soon, this would all be over. Back to her life, back to *alone*.

As if he read her thoughts, he pulled her into his arms, her back to his chest, into the shelter and out of the storm.

19

SILENCE FELL BETWEEN Nicole and Constantine as they prepared to leave the hotel room they'd called a safe zone for two weeks. The storm had long ago passed, danger had calmed as the hotel remained a secure hideaway. Knowing Flores was the leak had allowed communication to flow between her and her boss. Meanwhile, she and Constantine didn't speak as they packed what few things they had to take with them. There was so much to say, yet they said nothing at all.

They'd made love the night before. It had been passionate, heartfelt, perfect. She'd never felt this kind of connection to another person in her life. It was invigorating, exciting, scary as hell. She'd truthfully seen herself as a loner for the rest of her life, and perhaps she'd seen that in Constantine when she'd met him. What happened when two loners came together?

She didn't know. Maybe she needed to go home and find out if this was real. But there was no denying the idea that leaving this room and never feeling this way again burned a hole in her gut.

This was the first time she'd felt she belonged with a man. A man who, only weeks ago, she would have claimed was everything she didn't want. It was insane, yes, but she was done running from her feelings. She'd come to a conclusion: living to prove what she wasn't wasn't living at all.

In fact, over the past few weeks, she'd done a world of soul-searching, but clarity had come only the night before, as she stared at the ceiling, unable to sleep. She'd been living a lie her entire life, trying to be something she wasn't all to prove something to herself, and to the people she knew. She had to make changes. Which meant, she had to go home, convict Alvarez and then decide where that left her. What she didn't know was where Constantine fit in to those changes.

Done with her packing, Nicole sat down on the bed. She wore a blouse, jeans and tennis shoes, but soon she would be back to business attire. Today, she had awakened next to Constantine; tomorrow, they would be prosecutor and FBI agent, pretending to be strangers, on their best behavior for the jury. This was the end of the line. Their worlds would separate, perhaps forever.

Constantine zipped up a leather bag he'd bought from the hotel boutique and set it by the door. "Ready?"

The truth was that she wasn't sure she was ready at all, but she had no choice. She managed a nod, her gaze doing a quick sweep of his body in the process, lingering on his muscular thighs beneath the tight jeans he wore. The man was the caviar of denim. He made it sexy. But then, everything about him was sexy to her.

She drew a breath, knowing there was something she owed him—a confession of sorts. Her wish to pretend she was something she wasn't had made her blame him for things he had nothing to do with.

Not giving herself time to back out, she exhaled and blurted her declaration. "Back at the docks, I wanted Carlos dead."

Constantine didn't move, didn't appear to quite know what to say. "And you blamed me for making you feel that way."

"Yes," she whispered, her chest constricted. "How did you know?"

"The way you looked at me and then the way you couldn't look at me."

"I'm sorry," she said, feeling the odd pinch of tears in the back of her eyes. She never cried and she didn't want to now.

"It was human, Nicole. An instinct to survive."

He was so close, only a foot away, but right now so very distant emotionally. "I know. I've spent a lot of time trying to make up for the past, afraid of becoming what I was back then."

"And I scared you. I walk a line you don't want to walk. You think I'll change that. Make you like me." His jaw flexed. "I get that." The words held bitterness, a bite that hurt.

Nicole surged to her feet. "No. It's not like that."

"It is, Nicole." He hesitated, his jaw flexing. "We both know the limits between us. We simply stopped talking about them. Regardless of what you think, I'm not a cold-blooded killer, or Alvarez wouldn't be awaiting trial. But will I kill to save lives? Will I make a decision you might not feel fits your moral fiber? Yes."

How had this conversation gone so wrong? "I don't think you're a killer!" She took a step toward him, desperate to right this.

He held up a staying hand and she stopped. "You're going back to your perfectly planned life," he said, "free of bad influences like myself. I brought you into this thing with Carlos, and I will see you through it. I'll get you your life back. You have my word."

He grabbed the bags and reached for the door, pulling it open without giving her the chance to respond and tell him that what she really wanted was…him.

CONSTANTINE SPENT most of the ride to Austin in a foul mood, aware of her every move, her every sound. She drove him crazy with desire, with anger, with frustration. With…something more. Something he didn't want to think about. But he couldn't deny he had feelings for Nicole, nor could he deny how wrong he was for her.

He wasn't a man who lived within a structured set of rules. Nicole survived by creating control, which meant rules. He didn't think she was happy in that world, not for a minute, but it didn't matter. He wouldn't live as the man who made her question herself. His life had been danger and darkness, and regardless of his decision to leave the agency, he wasn't likely to change. He'd find trouble; he always did.

Nicole was upset now, but she'd get over it when she settled into her life. He knew all the psych workups. People fell hard for those who protected them, who they depended on. Right now, she would find a way to justify the things about him that were not quite right for her world, but later…later she would see more clearly. There was no reason to make this hard for either of them. He had to take this back to business, back to the place where this started, and ended. It was the right thing to do. Right. So why did his gut have knots the size of Texas?

He glanced at a street sign, estimating they were about a mile from their destination. Breaking the silence, he cast her a sideways look. "A team of agents will be waiting for our arrival," he explained matter-of-factly. "They have the entire top floor of the Four Seasons Hotel blocked off with special security. They still have nothing on Carlos. He's vanished."

"You'll be there, right? Not just this FBI team?"

The hopeful quality in her voice tightened those knots in his gut a bit more. "I told you I'd get you through this, and I meant it."

She drew a heavy breath and exhaled, her response cold. "I have the utmost confidence in your ability, Agent Vega."

Damn, he hated this. He shouldn't reach out to her but found himself softly saying, "Nicole. I'll still be near, still be by your side. I'm not going anywhere."

She didn't look at him. "Okay."

Son of a bitch. He didn't know what to do here. He wanted to comfort her. Hell, he wanted her in his bed. But he also knew what was best, knew she'd thank him later for this. So why wasn't this easy?

He grabbed the phone and called in, directing the car to the side entrance of the hotel. In a matter of minutes, they were being shuffled to a private elevator. Constantine grabbed Nicole's arm, wishing he could pull her close, but settling for keeping her within his grasp. They had appearances to keep up now, a jury to satisfy. He also had her safety to consider, and he trusted no one but himself to protect her. He was keeping her close, period.

Standing beside him, staring up at the blinking display of passing floors, she didn't look at him, but he felt her relax, felt her relief at his nearness. If he did nothing else for Nicole, he made her feel safe. That was something, at least.

His hand never left her arm as they stepped into the hall and traveled to the end of a long corridor. He let her go only when an agent opened the suite they would call home during the trial. He entered directly behind her.

In the center of the small living area, Agent-in-Charge Nelson waited. An ex-military man, he wore his hair buzzed; his suit, pressed perfectly.

He nodded at Constantine, a look of respect in his eyes. "Good to see you arrived safely." His attention turned to Nicole, and he offered her his hand. "Agent Nelson."

Nicole took his hand for a brief moment. "Thanks for your help while we were out there," she said. "How does this all work?"

"There are three bedrooms here. I put you in the one to the left. It's bigger and nicer. Your boss dropped off some papers for your review. You'll find them on the dresser."

"Okay," she said. "Thanks."

Nelson continued, "We'll want you in a controlled environment as much as possible, so only your direct family and people related to the case can visit on a limited basis. I need a list of anyone who might be allowed in, so we can check them out. If they aren't on that list, they don't get in. You'll have two agents, in addition to Agent Vega, at all times." His gaze flickered to Constantine. "After what happened with Flores, I don't blame him for not trusting anyone." He spoke directly to Constantine then. "We arrested him last night. He's been asking to talk to you."

"The day hell freezes over would be too soon."

"Did he say why he did it?" Nicole asked.

"Threatened his family," Nelson said, giving her a

quick look. "But we have procedures in place to handle those things. I suspect we'll discover it was more about money."

"Money is a powerful drug," she murmured softly, and Constantine knew she was thinking about her past. She'd told him how her father's firm wanted the big billing cases, no worry about what lowlifes they defended. "Can I go to my apartment to get some things?"

"I'm afraid I can't allow that. I can have a female agent pick up some things for you."

"Thank you." She hesitated. "Now, I'd better get on those papers that Dean left."

"Let me know if you need anything," Nelson said.

She inclined her head but didn't comment, nor did she look at Constantine. It took every ounce of willpower he had not to follow her with his eyes as she left the room.

He focused on Nelson. "Why don't we have Carlos yet?"

"We're trying."

"Not good enough. She'll never be safe if we don't get him. He'll hunt her down to prove a point. That he can get to someone I've been protecting."

"That he can get to you, and anyone near you, like you did him," Nelson returned accurately.

A muscle in his jaw jumped. "Yes. He won't kill me. He'll kill anyone near me. That means she's in real danger. I'm protecting her, so he'll want to prove he can kill her."

"And if you walk away from her?"

"It's too late," he said grimly. "He's got her in his sights."

"I'll start the relocation process. You want to talk to her or shall I?"

"Neither, damn it," Constantine said. "Get Carlos."

Nelson paused, then said, "I know you don't trust me—"

"I don't trust anyone at this point. It's not personal, man. This is the end of the road for me. I'm done after this. I plan to leave alive."

"You sure that's what you want? We need you."

He was sure. Damn sure. When the time came, he was ready to walk away from the Bureau without ever looking back. Why did he think walking away from Nicole wouldn't be that easy?

20

NICOLE ENTERED the Austin hotel suite after a long day in court, ever aware of Constantine behind her, beside her, near her—there, but not there. Watchful, but distant.

She walked straight to her room, edgy, ready to turn and demand they clear the air. But they weren't alone. They were never alone. Besides, he'd made his position clear. Their relationship was over. They were fire and ice. He wanted fire and apparently thought she wanted ice.

She found the door to her room and quickly shut herself inside, letting her briefcase slide to the floor. She leaned back against the closed door, her head resting on the wooden surface, eyes closed.

Constantine had been right about her perfectly planned life. She'd built a glass house. So perfect there was nothing real inside. There was laughter—no happiness. Just her own need to prove she wasn't defined by the past.

But back in Houston with Constantine, she had found what was missing. She'd gotten a taste of what it meant to share her life with someone else and she greedily wanted more. And more meant Constantine.

She inhaled, recognizing her emotions were turbulent at best and not all because of her relationship with Constantine. Her father's presence in the courtroom that day had messed with her head. He'd sat there, a judgmental look on his face. But no matter how flawed he might want to find her performance, he wouldn't be able to, and he only wanted to because she was doing work he didn't approve of. She was at the top of her game, performing her best. She wanted Alvarez put away, and she was going to make it happen. Her one regret was that she couldn't truly share the progress with Constantine, that they had to act as strangers for the sake of appearance. But they'd come too far to allow an affair to destroy credibility. They couldn't risk that getting out to the press, and maybe, inadvertently, the jury.

However, she wasn't going to be a wilting wallflower hiding in her room. She'd go out there, claim the desk and start working. Let Constantine hide in his room. She was done hiding. From herself. From her life. From him. Time to forgive herself. Time to stop wallowing in guilt. *Choose my own battles.* That idea had been working a number on her mind. Maybe she'd open her own law firm. She wasn't sure yet, but change was in the air for her. She was brave in the courtroom. Now she wanted to be brave beyond it.

No more hiding.

CONSTANTINE SAT IN his bedroom with the door open, listening to Nicole talk to one of the agents in the living area of the suite. Her voice trickled along his nerve endings, taunting him with what he wanted, what he couldn't have—her.

Staying away from her was killing him. Many times he'd considered saying to hell with putting some distance between them. No, he didn't fit into her prim-and-proper life, but he was convinced she didn't fit into that life, either. In fact, he'd convinced himself that throwing her over his shoulder and carrying her away from all of this would be best for her. He also knew Nicole had to see for herself, had to decide what was right for herself. Except now, she didn't have choices. Not after the news he'd gotten today. He scrubbed his jaw, dreading the conversation they had to have.

He shoved off the bed and walked to the doorway, leaning on the edge of the door frame. She stood behind the bar, pouring herself a Diet Sprite over ice, her gaze lifting to his as if she sensed his presence.

"We need to talk," he said. He motioned with his head, indicating his room. "In private."

Surprise flashed in her face. Not once since their return had they been alone. Her room was on the opposite side of the suite, their relationship strictly business to all those around them. Oh, but he could imagine being in bed with her, the sheets gone, his body all that covered her.

"Of course," she said, setting down her soda can and crossing the room, closing the distance. He watched her walk, her hips swaying in the velour sweats she'd bought back in Houston. Damn, how he wanted to lose himself in her. His zipper area expanded painfully, his body taut with the day's worth of desire that had gone unattended.

He backed up, letting her enter the room, shutting the door behind her. She walked to the bed and sat down. The bed. The place he wanted her. He leaned against the wall, crossing his arms over his chest. "We picked up one of Carlos's men today."

She gave him a cautious look. "I assume that's good, but you aren't acting like it is."

"He had some information. A message for me." He hesitated, hating this so damn much. "About you."

Her chin tilted downward. "And?"

"Anyone I get close to, he'll kill. Starting with you."

"No one knows about us."

"You're under my protection and have been. That's enough for him."

She blinked, swallowed and turned away. "And my family?"

"Alvarez wants this trial to end, so anything done to anyone that might cause a mistrial is still a risk. If something happened to your family, no doubt you'd have trouble going on. After this is over, Carlos will focus on me. That means he'll come for you."

She looked at him then. "But you can't be certain he won't go after my family."

"Not one hundred percent." He wished he could tell her otherwise. "You have no option but to go into a relocation program until Carlos is captured."

Her eyes went wide. "Oh, no," she said, rock-hard determination in her voice. "Not a chance." She pushed to her feet. "If there is one thing I have learned from all of this, it's that I'm tired of running. I ran to where I am now, to hide from what I was in the past. And I can't ask my family to give up their lives. Not that they will. They could die while I'm off hiding."

Uncrossing his arms, he pushed off the wall, going to stand in front of her, barely containing the urge to reach for her. "This is about staying alive, Nicole. I know it's hard but—"

"Would *you* run?"

What could he say to that? "My job is to hunt down criminals and capture them."

"Then do it now. Capture him. You said you'd make this go away."

He had promised. "I'm stuck in here or I would. I will." His hands went to her arms. "Nicole, baby—"

She shoved his arms away, a fierce frown on her face. "Don't 'Nicole baby' me, now. You haven't touched me in days. Don't use our fling as a form of manipulation."

"It's not like that. I wouldn't do that."

"*Not* like that. Then how is it? We've hardly said two words to each other since we returned, and now that you want me to do something your way, you pull out the 'baby' stuff?"

"Everything I've done, I've done to protect you."

She made a disbelieving sound. "This doesn't feel like protection. It feels like…" Her words trailed off, her lashes lowered, a few seconds ticked by. Her lashes lifted again and she gazed directly into his eyes. "The bottom line here is this. I'm not running anymore. Not from my past, not from Carlos. Catch him. Use me as bait. Do whatever. But I'm not going into hiding."

"I won't use you as bait."

"I want this over, Constantine. Even if I agree to hide, my family won't. My father has some 'man of steel' complex—I can't let them walk around with a bull's-eye on their backs because of me. If you won't use me to put an end to this, someone at the Bureau will." She narrowed her eyes on him, throwing out her dare. "So you decide. Will you use me or let someone else?" She tried to walk past him, and he maneuvered in front of her.

"No," he said. "I won't allow it. No one is using you as bait. I got you into this and I'll get you out."

They stared at one another, her lips parted, the world

somehow separating them, when only a few days before it had pulled them together.

"I got me into this by taking this case," she finally said. "*I'll* get me out of it."

She sidestepped him and this time he let her go, turning around to watch her leave. "Nicole," he said, as she reached for the door. Looking back over her shoulder, her gaze sought his, a question in her eyes.

"This isn't over," Constantine stated.

Tension charged the air, seconds passing by before she turned and left, the door shutting behind her.

Constantine sat down on the bed and pounded the mattress. Time and time again, those he cared about ended up hurt. He had to make this go away. Had to protect Nicole. The idea of something happening to her destroyed him. Damn it, he didn't want to care about her. But he did. And no matter how hard he tried to run from that fact, he couldn't. He was in love with Nicole.

THE NEXT AFTERNOON, Nicole finished up a long day in court. Nasty details that should have been revealed to the jury had been suppressed and then manipulated by the defense; Nicole's frustration over the judge's decision was high.

She walked toward the exit, Constantine waiting for her, leaning against the back wall, watchful. He wore black slacks, a black dress shirt and tie, his hair pulled back. He even made dress clothes look dangerous and sexy, and right now she hated him for it. To say she was intensely aware of him would be an understatement. Every inch of her body screamed with arousal when she looked at him. Anger and hurt did nothing to dispel the feeling. She was all for fighting battles, all for standing up and making a difference, but for once, she'd thought she wouldn't be doing it alone. She'd been wrong. And she wished she'd never felt that "together" feeling— how do you miss what you don't know?

Constantine grabbed the door for her, and for an instant their eyes met. Her stomach fluttered, and she quickly averted her gaze. By the time she slid into the back of an unmarked car with him, their knees brushing together, Nicole was ready to come unglued. She shivered despite herself—with want, with emotion.

Another agent started to slide in on the opposite side of the backseat, and Constantine held up a hand. In other words, "go away." The agent nodded and did as ordered, shutting them into the backseat. Alone. A tinted glass window gave them privacy from the driver. She turned to him, surprised at his actions, not sure what to expect. The drive was short, a mere two blocks. But she didn't have to guess his intentions for long.

Suddenly, she was in those big, strong arms, warmth surrounding her, his lips slanting over hers, tongue delving into her mouth with possessive heat. Passion and emotion washed over her, taking control, stealing her breath.

When the kiss ended all too soon, Nicole stared up at him, searching his dark eyes, eyes she could lose herself in for a lifetime. Eyes telling her he cared. A knock sounded on the window and she jumped. The short ride was over. No. They needed more time.

"One minute," Constantine called, his attention never leaving Nicole. "I *have* to know you're okay."

She didn't ask why. The kiss, the look in his eyes, the way she felt in his arms, told her everything. He cared. He hadn't shut her out. "Then stay with me."

His eyes softened a second before another knock sounded. They had to get out and pretend to be strangers again, at least until the trial was over.

Constantine brushed his cheek against hers and whispered her name. Nothing more. The next thing she knew, the door was opening, and with regret, she followed Constantine out of the backseat. Distant, but not nearly as distant as before.

She entered the hotel room a few minutes later filled with the warmth of knowing she and Constantine were finding their way back to each other. Their shared glances, as they decided to order a pizza instead of room service, were so hot, she didn't know how the other agents could miss the sizzle. But she didn't care. The trial was almost over, and these guys hated Alvarez. They wouldn't work against her. They'd been rooting for her in court.

Waiting for the pizza, she sat down on the couch and wrote down notes for her closing statements to review with her team. The two agents on duty played poker on the desk. Constantine took a call from someone, went to his room a few minutes to talk, then to her surprise, returned, no longer avoiding her. He took over a nearby chair and studied a security report that Agent Nelson sent him each evening.

When a knock came at the door, her stomach grumbled hungrily. "Yes!" she said, setting down her papers, preparing to get a soda.

But the agent didn't return with pizza. Instead, he returned with an awkward look on his face. He glanced at Constantine and then Nicole. "You have a visitor," he informed her. "Mike Parker. He's on the list. Says he's, ah, your husband."

"Ex-husband," she corrected, eyeing Constantine. He was already on his feet, his jaw set tight, eyes averted from hers. This was *so* not good. Her heart felt as if it had slipped to her stomach.

"Let him in?" the agent queried.

Reconciled to her situation, she nodded at the agent. "Let him in."

A few seconds later, Mike entered, dressed in designer dress slacks and a starched button-down shirt. Blond hair, blue eyes and a million-dollar, prep-school, fake smile were a few of the traits he used to manipulate people, both in and out of the courtroom.

He flashed her one of those smiles. "Good to see you, Nicole." The words held the hint of flirtation that he couldn't seem to speak to a woman without using.

She didn't invite him to sit down. "What can I do for you, Mike?" she asked, her cold tone reserved for him. Coldness meant to repulse his advances. He'd never stopped looking at her as his possession and tried to assert his claim every chance he could. Keeping him at a distance was her best defense.

Mike's gaze traveled to the table where the two agents played cards and then settled over her shoulder— to where Constantine stood, a flash of discomfort showing on his face; most people wouldn't notice, but she knew Mike better than she wanted to. Inwardly, she smiled, enjoying his discomfiture.

With a slow slide, Mike returned his attention to Nicole, acting unaffected by Constantine. A lie. He was good at those. "Watched you in court today," he said. "You looked good." He winked and glanced at her wrist. "See you still wear the bracelet I gave you for good luck."

The air crackled with tension. Willpower, pure and simple, was all that kept her from turning and explaining. She wore the bracelet as a reminder of what she never wanted to be again—either as an attorney or as a person. But Constantine would think otherwise. He would think she still cared for Mike—or worse, for her old life.

She swallowed hard, desperate to be rid of Mike and explain to Constantine. "Cut to the chase, Mike. What do you want?"

His lips twisted a bit. "Your father asked me to talk to you."

Figured. "So talk."

He glanced over her shoulder again and then back to her. "Can we do this alone?"

She considered declining but decided she'd better hear Mike out. "Fine," she said, pushing to her feet and heading to the bedroom, her gaze seeking Constantine, who was entering his own room.

Mike followed her into her room and tried to shut the door. She pointed to it. "Oh, no. It stays open." He grimaced, but left it open.

Nicole crossed her arms and turned to face him. "Now talk."

He was close, too close, but backing away more would make him feel powerful, as if he had intimidated her. And since he got off on intimidation, that would only drag this out further.

"Your father didn't send me," he announced. "I simply thought it past time we talked. You ran off over some outbreak of conscience. I get it that you felt you had to, but it's time to end this little emotional relay you're running. Now you've gone and put your family

in danger." He took a step toward her and she countered
with a step backward.

An evil smile formed on his lips at her actions as he
continued, "You're going to win this case, and it's a
masterpiece of a win. You'll pay back whatever debt you
feel you owe society by putting Alvarez away. It's done.
You can come home again."

"We're divorced! And, my God, you must think I am
stupid," she said. "You and Daddy planned this, didn't
you? An effort to put the firm in the spotlight by way
of the press I'm getting."

He moved quickly then, grabbing her before she
knew his intentions. "You took the perfect life and threw
it in the trash," he said, pulling her against his body. "I
work for your father. I am supposed to be married to
you. Have your affairs, have a separate life, but stop
tearing apart the core of this family."

"You and I are not the core of anything!" She
shoved at his chest. "Get off me or I swear I will get
all three of those agents to make you leave."

"It'll only take one." Nicole looked up at the sound of
Constantine's voice, thick with danger, his attention fixed
on Mike, as he added, "You have no idea how badly I
want to hurt you right now, so I suggest you let go of her."

Mike didn't let go, possessiveness in his rebuttal.
"Touch me and I'll sue."

"If you live."

Mike let go. He stepped back as if burned. And
Nicole didn't blame him. Something in Constantine's
words, his presence, oozed downright menace. "Leave,"
Constantine said.

Mike headed toward the door. Constantine eased
back enough for Mike to pass…barely.

Constantine faced Nicole. "You also have no idea," he said, his words taut, "how much *I hate* the idea of that pencil-neck, preppy lowlife touching you. But you know what I hate even more? I hate that you wear *his* bracelet."

And then he was gone, leaving her to gape after him. She couldn't lose Constantine over Mike. Couldn't. Wouldn't. Mike was nothing. Constantine was everything. Constantine was… She loved him. She loved him so very much.

She didn't think anymore; instead Nicole stormed out of her room—unconcerned about the other agents' noticing her—with one destination in her sights. Constantine's bedroom.

21

NICOLE DIDN'T BOTHER to knock before charging into Constantine's room. She slammed the door shut and leaned against it, hands flat on the wooden surface behind her, her chest heaving with anxiety.

Constantine sat on the bed, face buried in his hands. He looked up at her. "Go away, Nicole. We have nothing to talk about."

His words cut through her with the sharpness of a blade. "Mike means nothing to me."

He ran his hand over his thigh. "I don't want to hear this." Pain dripped from his words, although he tried to appear cold, as cold as she had been to Mike.

She didn't want Constantine to hurt, but at least she knew he cared. She darted toward him then, falling to her knees in front of him, and put her hands on his muscular thighs. Touching him. Touching him felt right. "I wear the bracelet to remind me of what I never want to become again. To remind me that no matter how bad it gets in court, I am not like him."

In response, he distanced himself from her—no sign of him reaching for her. His eyes were black ice. "That you need that reminder says everything," he whispered. "Your past defines who you are."

She ripped the bracelet from her arm. "I don't need the

bracelet. I'm done running from the past. I'm done letting it define me. I'm resigning from my job. I'm going to start fresh. I need to start fresh. And I want to do it with you."

Surprise flashed in his face. A hint of hope. Then it was gone; the coldness, back. "Until I do something that makes you question yourself, or maybe my intentions. Something that has you painting me as a bad influence."

"No." How could she get through to him? At this point, proclaiming her love would fall on deaf ears. He believed she had a negative opinion of him and, on some level, didn't trust him. She recalled a conversation they'd had back in Houston—she knew what to do.

Her eyes traveled the room, looking for the tool she sought before pushing to her feet. At the window, she tugged away the sashes holding the curtains and returned to her prior position, on her knees, in front of him.

Nicole stared up at him, hoping he saw the truth in her eyes as she spoke. "I believe in you. I *trust* you." She held out the sashes. "Tie me up, Constantine. You know I wouldn't let you if I didn't completely trust you. Be the first. Be the last. Be the only one."

A look of disbelief crossed his face. "What?"

She repeated her words, eager to make them take root in his mind. "You said I wouldn't let you tie me up until I trusted you completely. I do. I… Constantine." She drew a deep breath for courage. "I have no idea how you feel about me, but I—"

And then she was in his arms. He lay back on the mattress, pulling her with him. A second later, she was the one on her back, Constantine's big body on top of her, kissing her, devouring her with passion and warmth.

Long moments later, he tore his lips from hers. "You want to know how I feel about you?" he asked, staring down at her. "I love you, Nicole. I love you with all of my heart."

Her arms wrapped around his neck, her heart swelling with joy. "I love you, too. I love you so much."

Tenderness filled his face. "Then *do* run away. Run away with me, Nicole. Take a year off from work, and travel the world. With me. We'll be careful. Carlos won't be able to follow us."

Her mind was still reeling from the "take a year off and travel the world" statement, when he spoke again.

"It'll work, *cariña*. If we're lucky, he'll be in custody by the time you and I hit our first destination. Nelson is waiting for a yes, and then he'll coordinate everything. So say yes."

Everything was falling into place. "I… Yes. Okay." Her fingers brushed a strand of hair out of his eyes. "But I can't just run off for a year, as wonderful as that sounds. I have to figure out what is next for me. Maybe my own firm. I have some money, but—"

He grabbed her hand tenderly and kissed it. When they were intimate, he did that often, and she loved it. "Forget money," he said. "I told you, I have money. For travel, for whatever you need."

"I can't forget money." Working as a public servant didn't allow her much saving, and taking money from her father meant working for him, which would never happen again.

"If money weren't an issue, would you take the year and enjoy it?"

"Yes, but—"

He kissed her. And kissed her some more. By the

time his lips left hers, she ached with need, and couldn't remember what they had been talking about. But he did. "Money isn't an issue," he declared. "We'll leave the day the trial ends."

She didn't consider arguing. She loved him and he, her, and she believed in that for the first time in her life. "All right, then," Nicole whispered. Somehow she still held the sashes in her hands. She smiled. "Want to tie me up to seal the deal?"

"Later," he murmured huskily. "Now I just want to make love to you, Nicole. Nice and slow." And he kissed her again, starting with her lips and then exploring, tasting, loving, until she shivered with release. And then he started all over again.

THREE DAYS LATER Nicole stood in the courtroom. She was ecstatic as she heard the jury's guilty verdict for every charge against Alvarez. Deliberation had taken a mere four hours. This was a victory Nicole felt on so many levels that she wanted to dance with joy. Next up would be Flores, but her boss was handling that one.

The minute she broke free of the chaos that followed the court's adjournment, her eyes found Constantine's, sharing a silent look of happiness with him. They'd done it. Alvarez would never hurt anyone again.

As for Carlos, the Bureau had tracked him down through an informant and executed the arrest perfectly.

Reporters and flashing cameras awaited them outside on the courtroom steps, and Nicole gave a short statement. Not soon enough, it was over, and she slid into the passenger seat of a car, Constantine by her side.

Nicole and her family would be safe. Everything about Constantine's plan had fallen into place.

Nicole couldn't wait to get to Greece—the pictures in the ads had been gorgeous. For once, she was living for the pure thrill of it, taking chances, and loving it.

Constantine held her hand as he drove the car away. Nicole smiled at him. Smiled because she was embarking on a new adventure, and she couldn't wait to see what came next.

She was happy.

Epilogue

NICOLE LAY TIED to a massive bed with fluffy white linens, ensconced within the massive walls of the Greek villa that Constantine had rented for an extended stay. A month, maybe two. Then they would be off to a new destination.

A breeze blew in through the open patio doors, the sheer white drapes of the bedposts billowing with its cool touch. They were celebrating their future with champagne, chocolate and a game of sensual play.

Even further cause for celebration, Nicole's sister had seen the light in the midst of all the darkness. She was going to travel for a while, with some hot man she had met in Hawaii, and then decide what was next. Nicole even thought they might open a law firm together. They'd both return from exploring the world and get back to work.

Right now though, there was only one thing Nicole wanted to explore. Constantine stood at the foot of the bed, gloriously naked and erect—a temptation she couldn't touch. Her body ached with a burn only he could soothe. He devoured her with his eyes, and the result was remarkably arousing.

"Please come here," she whispered hoarsely.

"Impatient?" he asked, teasing her with his voice.

"Yes. And please remember whatever you do to me, I intend to return tenfold."

He laughed, the sound deep and sultry. His knees came down on the mattress, his hands spreading her thighs, until he lowered his shoulders between them. A warm trickle of breath touched her core, and she gasped.

She would have cried out for more, but his hands possessively moved over her hips and then, out of nowhere, a velvet box appeared on her stomach.

Her breath lodged in her throat. Was that what she thought it was? He kissed her stomach and peered up at her. "Say you'll marry me, and I'll let you see what's inside."

"You want to marry me?"

"More than anything in this world."

"Yes," she murmured, tears forming in her eyes. "I love you. Of course, I'll marry you."

He smiled and flipped open the top of the box. She blinked. She struggled to find her voice. "It's...the most amazing diamond I've ever seen in my life. Take it back. It's too much money." He was FBI, and investments or not, he couldn't have that kind of money. Was he trying to impress her? "I don't need a fancy ring. I just need you."

Her head was spinning. She couldn't believe this. It was like a fairy tale.

"Now," Constantine murmured. "Where was I? Ah, yes." His hands caressed their way down the sides of her body then rested on her breasts. "I believe I was in the process of making you beg."

And as he slid back to that hotspot he'd warmed with his breath only minutes before, she was pretty darn sure, he would succeed. Only, for once, giving away the control didn't mean giving away a part of herself. It simply meant sharing.

And pleasure. Lots of pleasure.

* * * * *

*Celebrate 60 years of pure reading pleasure
with Harlequin® Books!*

*Harlequin Romance® is celebrating
by showering you with*
DIAMOND BRIDES
*in February 2009.
Six stories that promise to bring a touch
of sparkle to your life,
with diamond proposals and dazzling weddings,
sparkling brides and gorgeous grooms!*

Enjoy a sneak peek at Caroline Anderson's
TWO LITTLE MIRACLES,
*available February 2009
from Harlequin Romance®*

"I'VE FOUND HER."

Max froze.

It was what he'd been waiting for since June, but now—now he was almost afraid to voice the question. His heart stalling, he leaned slowly back in his chair and scoured the investigator's face for clues. "Where?" he asked, and his voice sounded rough and unused, like a rusty hinge.

"In Suffolk. She's living in a cottage."

Living. His heart crashed back to life, and he sucked in a long, slow breath. All these months he'd feared—

"Is she well?"

"Yes, she's well."

He had to force himself to ask the next question. "Alone?"

The man paused. "No. The cottage belongs to a man called John Blake. He's working away at the moment, but he comes and goes."

God. He felt sick. So sick he hardly registered the next few words, but then gradually they sank in. "She's got *what?*"

"Babies. Twin girls. They're eight months old."

"Eight—" he echoed under his breath. "They must be his."

He was thinking out loud, but the P.I. heard and corrected him.

"Apparently not. I gather they're hers. She's been there since mid-January last year, and they were born during the summer—June, the woman in the post office thought. She was more than helpful. I think there's been a certain amount of speculation about their relationship."

He'd just bet there had. God, he was going to kill her. Or Blake. Maybe both of them.

"Of course, looking at the dates, she was presumably pregnant when she left you, so they could be yours, or she could have been having an affair with this Blake character before…"

He glared at the unfortunate P.I. "Just stick to your job. I can do the math," he snapped, swallowing the unpalatable possibility that she'd been unfaithful to him before she'd left. "Where is she? I want the address."

"It's all in here," the man said, sliding a large envelope across the desk to him. "With my invoice."

"I'll get it seen to. Thank you."

"If there's anything else you need, Mr. Gallagher, any further information—"

"I'll be in touch."

"The woman in the post office told me Blake was away at the moment, if that helps," he added quietly, and opened the door.

Max stared down at the envelope, hardly daring to open it, but when the door clicked softly shut behind the P.I., he eased up the flap, tipped it and felt his breath jam in his throat as the photos spilled out over the desk.

Oh, Lord, she looked gorgeous. Different, though. It took him a moment to recognize her, because she'd grown her hair, and it was tied back in a ponytail, making her look younger and somehow freer. The blond highlights were gone, and it was back to its natural soft golden-brown, with a little curl in the end of the ponytail that he wanted to thread his fingers through and tug, just gently, to draw her back to him.

Crazy. She'd put on a little weight, but it suited her. She looked well and happy and beautiful, but oddly, considering how desperate he'd been for news of her for the past year—one year, three weeks and two days, to be exact—it wasn't only Julia who held his attention after the initial shock. It was the babies sitting side by side in a supermarket trolley. Two identical and absolutely beautiful little girls.

* * * * *

When Max Gallagher hires a P.I. to find his estranged wife, Julia, he discovers she's not alone— she has twin baby girls, and they might be his. Now workaholic Max has just two weeks to prove that he can be a wonderful husband and father to the family he wants to treasure.

Look for
TWO LITTLE MIRACLES
by Caroline Anderson,
available February 2009
from Harlequin Romance®

HARLEQUIN Romance®

This February the Harlequin® Romance series
will feature six Diamond Brides stories featuring
diamond proposals and gorgeous grooms.

Share your dream wedding proposal and you could WIN!

The most romantic entry will win a diamond
necklace and will inspire a proposal in one of
our upcoming Diamond Grooms books in 2010.

In 100 words or less, tell us the most romantic
way that you dream of being proposed to.

For more information, and to enter
the Diamond Brides Proposal contest, please visit
www.DiamondBridesProposal.com

Or mail your entry to us at:

IN THE U.S.: 3010 Walden Ave., P.O. Box 9069, Buffalo, NY 14269-9069
IN CANADA: 225 Duncan Mill Road, Don Mills, ON M3B 3K9

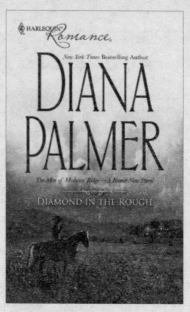

DIAMOND IN THE ROUGH

John Callister is a millionaire rancher, yet when he meets
lovely Sassy Peale and she thinks he's a cowboy, he goes along
with her misconception. He's had enough of gold diggers,
and this is a chance to be valued for himself, not his money.
But when Sassy finds out the truth, she feels John was merely
playing with her. John will have to convince her that he's truly
the man she fell in love with—a diamond in the rough.

THE MEN OF MEDICINE RIDGE—a brand-new miniseries
set in the wilds of Montana!

Available April 2009 wherever you buy books.

You're invited to join our Tell Harlequin Reader Panel!

By joining our new reader panel you will:

- Receive Harlequin® books—they are FREE and yours to keep with no obligation to purchase anything!
- Participate in fun online surveys
- Exchange opinions and ideas with women just like you
- Have a say in our new book ideas and help us publish the best in women's fiction

In addition, you will have a chance to win great prizes and receive special gifts!
See Web site for details. Some conditions apply.
Space is limited.

To join, visit us at
www.TellHarlequin.com.

REQUEST YOUR FREE BOOKS!

2 FREE NOVELS
PLUS 2
FREE GIFTS!

HARLEQUIN®

Blaze™

Red-hot reads!

HARLEQUIN *Blaze*™

COMING NEXT MONTH

#447 BLAZING BEDTIME STORIES Kimberly Raye, Leslie Kelly, Rhonda Nelson
Who said fairy tales are just for kids? Three intrepid Blaze heroines decide to take a break from reality—and discover, to their personal satisfaction, just how sexy happily-ever-afters can be....

#448 SOMETHING WICKED Julie Leto
Josie Vargas has always believed in love at first sight—and once she meets lawman Rick Fernandez, she's a goner. If only he didn't have those demons stalking him....

#449 THE CONCUBINE Jade Lee
Blaze Historicals
Chen Ji Yue has the chance to bring the ultimate honor to her family if she is chosen as one of the new emperor's wives. Of course, first she has to beat out the other three hundred virgins vying for the position. And then she has to stay out of the bed of Sun Bo Tao, the emperor's best friend.

#450 SHE THINKS HER EX IS SEXY... Joanne Rock
24 Hours: Lost
After a very public quarrel with her boyfriend, rock star Romeo Jinks, actress Shannon Leigh just wants to get her life back. But when she finds herself stranded in the Sonoran Desert with her ex, she learns that great sex can make breaking up hard to do.

#451 ABLE-BODIED Karen Foley
Uniformly Hot!
Delta Force operator Ransom Bennett is used to handling anything that comes his way. But debilitating headaches have put him almost out of action. Luckily, his new neighbor, Hannah Hartwell, knows how to handle his pain...and him, too.

#452 UNDER THE INFLUENCE Nancy Warren
Forbidden Fantasies
Sexy bartender Johnny Santini mixes one wicked martini. Or so business exec Natalie Fanshaw discovers, sitting at his bar one lonely Valentine's night. Could a fling with him be a recipe for disaster? Well, she could always claim to be under the influence....